NO FEAR SH

NO FEAR SHAKESPEARE

NO FEAR SHAKESPEARE

THE TEMPEST

Edited by
John Crowther

*sparknotes

SPARKNOTES and NO FEAR SHAKESPEARE
are registered trademarks of SparkNotes LLC.

Text © 2003 Sterling Publishing Co., Inc.

The original text and translation for this edition was prepared by John Crowther.

ISBN 978-1-58663-849-8

Library of Congress Cataloging-in-Publication Data
Shakespeare, William, 1564–1616.
  The tempest / edited by John Crowther.
     p. cm. — (No fear Shakespeare)
  Summary: Presents the original text of Shakespeare's play side by side
with a modern version, with marginal notes and explanations and full
descriptions of each character.
  ISBN 1-58663-849-1 (pbk.) ISBN 1-4114-0046-1 (hc.)
  1. Survival after airplane accidents, shipwrecks, etc.—Drama.
2. Fathers and daughters—Drama. 3. Young adult drama, English.
4. Magicians—Drama. 5. Islands—Drama. [1. Shakespeare, William,
1564–1616. Tempest. 2. Plays. 3. English literature—History and
criticism.] I. Crowther, John (John C.) II. Title.
PR2833.A25 2003
822.3'3—dc21   2003004311

Distributed in Canada by Sterling Publishing Co., Inc.
c/o Canadian Manda Group, 664 Annette Street
Toronto, Ontario M6S 2C8, Canada
Distributed in the United Kingdom by GMC Distribution Services
Castle Place, 166 High Street, Lewes, East Sussex BN7 1XU, England
Distributed in Australia by NewSouth Books
University of New South Wales, Sydney, NSW 2052, Australia

For information about custom editions, special sales, and premium and corporate purchases,
please contact Sterling Special Sales at 800-805-5489 or specialsales@sterlingpublishing.com.

Manufactured in Canada

Lot #:
46 48 50 49 47

06/20

sterlingpublishing.com
sparknotes.com

There's matter in these sighs, these profound heaves.
You must translate: 'tis fit we understand them.

(*Hamlet*, 4.1.1–2)

FEAR NOT.

Have you ever found yourself looking at a Shakespeare play, then down at the footnotes, then back at the play, and still not understanding? You know what the individual words mean, but they don't add up. SparkNotes' *No Fear Shakespeare* will help you break through all that. Put the pieces together with our easy-to-read translations. Soon you'll be reading Shakespeare's own words fearlessly—and actually enjoying it.

No Fear Shakespeare puts Shakespeare's language side-by-side with a facing-page translation into modern English— the kind of English people actually speak today. When Shakespeare's words make your head spin, our translation will help you sort out what's happening, who's saying what, and why.

THE TEMPEST

CHARACTERS

Prospero—The play's protagonist and Miranda's father. Twelve years before the events of the play, Prospero was the duke of Milan. His brother, Antonio, in concert with Alonso, king of Naples, usurped him, forcing him to flee in a boat with his daughter. The honest lord Gonzalo aided Prospero in his escape. Prospero has spent his twelve years on an island refining the magic that gives him the power he needs to punish and reconcile with his enemies.

Miranda—Prospero's daughter, whom he brought with him to the island when she was still a small child. Miranda has never seen any men other than her father and Caliban, although she dimly remembers being cared for by female servants as an infant. Because she has been sealed off from the world for so long, Miranda's perceptions of other people tend to be naïve and non-judgmental. She is compassionate, generous, and loyal to her father.

Ariel—Prospero's spirit helper, a powerful supernatural being whom Prospero controls completely. Rescued by Prospero from a long imprisonment (within a tree) at the hands of the witch Sycorax, Ariel is Prospero's servant until Prospero decides to release him. He is mischievous and ubiquitous, able to traverse the length of the island in an instant and change shapes at will. Ariel carries out virtually every task Prospero needs accomplished in the play.

Caliban—Another of Prospero's servants. Caliban, the son of the now-deceased witch Sycorax, acquainted Prospero with the island when Prospero arrived. Caliban believes that the island rightfully belongs to him and that Prospero stole it. Caliban's speech and behavior is sometimes coarse and brutal, sometimes eloquent and sensitive, as in his rebukes of Prospero in Act 1, scene 2, and in his description of the eerie beauty of the island.

Ferdinand—Son and heir of Alonso. Ferdinand seems in some ways to be as pure and naïve as Miranda. He falls in love with her upon first sight and happily submits to servitude in order to win Prospero's approval.

Alonso—King of Naples and father of Ferdinand. Alonso aided Antonio in unseating Prospero as duke of Milan twelve years before. Over the course of the play, Alonso comes to regret his past actions and desire a reconciliation with Prospero.

Antonio—Prospero's thoroughly wicked brother who betrayed Prospero's trust and stole his dukedom years before the play begins. Once on the island, Antonio wastes no time demonstrating that he is still power-hungry and murderous, persuading Sebastian to help him kill Alonso. Though Prospero forgives him at the end of the play, Antonio never repents for his misdeeds.

Sebastian—Alonso's brother. Like Antonio, Sebastian is wicked and underhanded. Antonio easily persuades him to agree to kill Alonso. Also like Antonio, Sebastian is unrepentant at the end of the play.

Gonzalo—An old, honest lord. The goodhearted Gonzalo helped Prospero and Miranda to escape and survive after Antonio usurped Prospero's title. During the play, Gonzalo does his best to cheer up the despondent Alonso, maintains an optimistic outlook on the island where they're standed, and remains unfazed by the insulting taunts of Antonio and Sebastian.

Trinculo and **Stefano**—Two minor members of the ship-wrecked party. Trinculo, a jester, and Stefano, a drunken butler, provide a comic foil to the other, more powerful pairs of Prospero and Alonso and Antonio and Sebastian. Their drunken boasting and petty greed reflect and deflate the quarrels and power struggles of Prospero and the other noblemen.

Boatswain—Appearing only in the first and last scenes, the Boatswain angers the noble characters with his foul-mouthed and rude remarks, but remains competent and resourceful in the shipwreck scene, demanding practical help rather than weeping and prayer.

THE
TEMPEST

ACT ONE
SCENE 1

A tempestuous noise of thunder and lightning heard
Enter a MASTER *and a* BOATSWAIN

MASTER
> Boatswain!

BOATSWAIN
> Here, master. What cheer?

MASTER
> Good, speak to th' mariners. Fall to 't yarely, or we run
> ourselves aground. Bestir, bestir.

Exit MASTER

Enter MARINERS

BOATSWAIN
5   Heigh, my hearts! Cheerly, cheerly, my hearts! Yare! Yare!
> Take in the topsail.—Tend to th' master's whistle.—Blow,
> till thou burst thy wind, if room enough!

Enter ALONSO, SEBASTIAN, ANTONIO, FERDINAND, GONZALO,
and others

ALONSO
> Good Boatswain, have care. Where's the Master?
> Play the men.

BOATSWAIN
10   I pray now, keep below.

ANTONIO
> Where is the Master, Boatswain?

ACT ONE

SCENE 1

Boatswain = Ship's officer in charge of the hull and other equipment. Pronounced "bósun"

Master = Captain

Loud noises of a storm with thunder and lightning.
A ship's MASTER *and* BOATSWAIN *enter.*

MASTER

Boatswain!

BOATSWAIN

I'm here, sir. How can I help you?

MASTER

My good boy, give the other sailors a pep talk—and do it fast, before we're shipwrecked. Hurry, hurry!

The MASTER *exits.*

SAILORS *enter.*

BOATSWAIN

Come on, men! That's the way to do it! Quickly! Quickly! Take in the upper sail. Listen to the master's orders. —Blow your heart out, storm! So long as we have enough room to avoid running aground!

ALONSO, SEBASTIAN, ANTONIO, FERDINAND, GONZALO, *and others enter.*

ALONSO

Be careful, good Boatswain! Where's the Master? Make these men work.

BOATSWAIN

Please stay below deck, sir.

ANTONIO

Where's the Master, Boatswain?

BOATSWAIN

Do you not hear him? You mar our labor. Keep your cabins.
You do assist the storm.

GONZALO

Nay, good, be patient.

BOATSWAIN

15   When the sea is. Hence! What cares these roarers for the
name of king? To cabin, silence! Trouble us not.

GONZALO

Good, yet remember whom thou hast aboard.

BOATSWAIN

None that I more love than myself. You are a councilor. If
you can command these elements to silence and work the
20   peace of the present, we will not hand a rope more. Use your
authority. If you cannot, give thanks you have lived so long
and make yourself ready in your cabin for the mischance of
the hour, if it so hap.—Cheerly, good hearts!—Out of our
way, I say.

Exit BOATSWAIN

GONZALO

25   I have great comfort from this fellow. Methinks he hath no
drowning mark upon him. His complexion is perfect
gallows. Stand fast, good Fate, to his hanging. Make the
rope of his destiny our cable, for our own doth little
advantage. If he be not born to be hanged, our case is
30   miserable.

Exeunt GONZALO *and courtiers*

BOATSWAIN

He's busy, can't you hear him giving orders? You're getting in the way of our work. Stay in your cabins. You're helping the storm, not us.

GONZALO

Don't get wound up, my good man.

BOATSWAIN

I'm only wound up because the sea's wound up. Now get out of here! Do you think these waves care anything about kings and officials? Go to your cabins and be quiet! Don't bother us up here.

GONZALO

Just remember who you've got on board with you, good man.

BOATSWAIN

Nobody I care about more than myself. You're a king's advisor. If you can order the storm to calm down, we can all put down our ropes and rest. Go ahead, use your authority. If you can't do it, be grateful you've lived this long and go wait to die in your cabin, if it comes to that.—Harder, men!—Now get out of our way, I'm telling you.

The BOATSWAIN *exits.*

GONZALO

Gonzalo implies that the Boatswain looks and acts like a dangerous criminal.

I feel a lot better after talking to this guy. He doesn't look like a person who would drown—he looks like he was born to be hanged. I hope he lives long enough to be hanged. The rope that hangs him will do more good than all the ropes on this ship, since it'll guarantee he stays alive through this storm. But if he's not destined to die by hanging, then our chances don't look too good.

GONZALO *exits with the other men of court.*

Enter BOATSWAIN

BOATSWAIN
Down with the topmast! Yare, lower, lower! Bring her to try
wi' th' main course.

A cry within

A plague upon this howling! They are louder than the
weather or our office.

Enter SEBASTIAN, ANTONIO, *and* GONZALO

35   Yet again? What do you here? Shall we give o'er and drown?
Have you a mind to sink?

SEBASTIAN
A pox o' your throat, you bawling, blasphemous,
incharitable dog!

BOATSWAIN
Work you, then.

ANTONIO
40   Hang, cur! Hang, you whoreson insolent noisemaker! We
are less afraid to be drowned than thou art.

GONZALO
I'll warrant him for drowning though the ship were no
stronger than a nutshell and as leaky as an unstanched
wench.

BOATSWAIN
45   Lay her a-hold, a-hold! Set her two courses off to sea again.
Lay her off!

Enter MARINERS, *wet*

MARINERS
All lost! To prayers, to prayers, all lost!

The BOATSWAIN *enters.*

BOATSWAIN

Bring down that top sail! Fast! Lower, lower! Let the ship sail close to the wind.

A shout offstage.

Damn those men shouting down there! They're louder than the storm or us sailors.

SEBASTIAN, ANTONIO, *and* GONZALO *enter.*

Oh, not you again. What do you want? Should we all give up and drown? Do you want to sink?

SEBASTIAN

Oh, go to hell, you loud-mouthed bastard!

BOATSWAIN

Well, get to work, then.

ANTONIO

Just die, you lowlife! Go ahead and die, you nasty, rude bastard! You're more scared of drowning than we are.

GONZALO

Yes, I guarantee he won't drown—even if this ship were as fragile as an eggshell and as leaky as a menstruating woman.

BOATSWAIN

Turn the ship to the wind! Set the sails and let her go out to sea again!

More SAILORS *enter, wet.*

SAILORS

It's no use! Pray for your lives! We're done for!

Exit MARINERS

BOATSWAIN
What, must our mouths be cold?

GONZALO
The king and prince at prayers. Let's assist them, for our
50   case is as theirs.

SEBASTIAN
I'm out of patience.

ANTONIO
We are merely cheated of our lives by drunkards. This
wide-chopped rascal—would thou mightst lie drowning
the washing of ten tides!

GONZALO
55   He'll be hanged yet, though every drop of water swear
against it and gape at widest to glut him.

A confused noise within

VOICES
(within) Mercy on us!—We split, we split!—Farewell, my
wife and children!—Farewell, brother!—We split, we
split, we split!

ANTONIO
60   Let's all sink wi' th' king.

SEBASTIAN
Let's take leave of him.

Exeunt ANTONIO *and* SEBASTIAN

The SAILORS *exit.*

BOATSWAIN

What, we're going to die?

GONZALO

The king and the prince are praying. Let's go join them, since whatever happens to them happens to us too.

SEBASTIAN

I'm out of patience.

ANTONIO

Yes, we've been cheated out of our lives by a bunch of drunken, incompetent sailors. This bigmouth jerk here—(*to* BOATSWAIN) I hope you drown ten times over!

GONZALO

He'll still die by hanging, not drowning, even if every drop of water in the sea tries to swallow him.

A confused noise offstage.

VOICES

God have mercy on us!—The ship's breaking up!— Goodbye, wife and kids!—Goodbye, brother!— We're breaking up, we're breaking up!

ANTONIO

Let's all sink with the king.

SEBASTIAN

Let's say goodbye to him.

ANTONIO *and* SEBASTIAN *exit.*

GONZALO
Now would I give a thousand furlongs of sea for an acre of
barren ground: long heath, brown furze, anything. The
wills above be done, but I would fain die a dry death.

Exeunt

GONZALO

1 furlong = 220 yards

Right now I'd give a thousand furlongs of sea for one little acre of dry ground: barren weed patch, anything at all. What's destined to happen will happen, but I'd give anything to be dry when I die.

They exit.

ACT 1, SCENE 2

Enter PROSPERO *and* MIRANDA

MIRANDA
If by your art, my dearest father, you have
Put the wild waters in this roar, allay them.
The sky, it seems, would pour down stinking pitch,
But that the sea, mounting to th' welkin's cheek,
5   Dashes the fire out. Oh, I have suffered
With those that I saw suffer. A brave vessel
Who had, no doubt, some noble creature in her
Dashed all to pieces. Oh, the cry did knock
Against my very heart! Poor souls, they perished.
10   Had I been any god of power, I would
Have sunk the sea within the earth or ere
It should the good ship so have swallowed and
The fraughting souls within her.

PROSPERO
                                    Be collected.
No more amazement. Tell your piteous heart
15   There's no harm done.

MIRANDA
                              Oh, woe the day!

PROSPERO
                                              No harm.
I have done nothing but in care of thee,
Of thee, my dear one—thee my daughter, who
Art ignorant of what thou art, naught knowing
Of whence I am, nor that I am more better
20   Than Prospero, master of a full poor cell
And thy no greater father.

MIRANDA
                            More to know
Did never meddle with my thoughts.

ACT 1, SCENE 2

PROSPERO *and* MIRANDA *enter.*

MIRANDA

Dear father, if you caused this terrible storm with your magic powers, please put an end to it. The sky's so dark it looks like it would rain down boiling hot tar if the sea weren't swelling up to the sky to put its fire out. Oh, I suffered along with all the men I watched suffer! A fine ship, with some good people in it, I'm sure, smashed to pieces. Their dying shouts broke my heart! The poor people died. If I'd been a god I would've let the sea sink inside the earth before it had a chance to swallow up that ship and all the people it was carrying.

PROSPERO

Calm down. There's nothing to get upset about. No harm was done.

MIRANDA

Oh, what a horrible day!

PROSPERO

There was no harm, I'm telling you. Everything I've done has been for you, my dear daughter. You don't know what you are, since you don't know who I am or where I come from, or that I'm better than merely Prospero, your humble father who lives in a poor little shack.

MIRANDA

It never occurred to me to imagine there was anything more to know.

PROSPERO
                                                    'Tis time
    I should inform thee farther. Lend thy hand
    And pluck my magic garment from me.

    MIRANDA *helps* PROSPERO *remove his mantle*

                                                    So,
25 Lie there, my art.—Wipe thou thine eyes. Have comfort.
    The direful spectacle of the wrack, which touched
    The very virtue of compassion in thee,
    I have with such provision in mine art
    So safely ordered that there is no soul—
30 No, not so much perdition as an hair
    Betid to any creature in the vessel—
    Which thou heard'st cry, which thou sawst sink. Sit down.
    For thou must now know farther.

MIRANDA
                                                    You have often
    Begun to tell me what I am, but stopped
35 And left me to a bootless inquisition,
    Concluding, "Stay. Not yet."

PROSPERO
                                            The hour's now come.
    The very minute bids thee ope thine ear.
    Obey and be attentive. Canst thou remember
    A time before we came unto this cell?
40 I do not think thou canst, for then thou wast not
    Out three years old.

MIRANDA
                                        Certainly, sir, I can.

PROSPERO
    By what? By any other house or person?
    Of anything the image tell me that
    Hath kept with thy remembrance.

PROSPERO

It's time for you to know the whole story. Give me a hand and help me off with this magic cloak.

MIRANDA *helps* PROSPERO *remove his cloak.*

(to the cloak) So, lie there, my magic. *(to* MIRANDA*)* Wipe your eyes. Take comfort. I arranged the horrible sight of this shipwreck, which moved you to such pity, so carefully that not a single person was hurt—no, not so much as a hair on anyone's head was destroyed in the ship that you saw sink. Sit down. It's time for you to know more. *(they sit)*

MIRANDA

You've often started to tell me who I am, but then suddenly stopped, leaving me asking questions that never get answered, telling me, "Wait. Not yet."

PROSPERO

Well, the time has come. This is the moment for you to listen hard and pay close attention. Can you remember the time before you came to live in this shack? I doubt it, since you weren't even three at the time.

MIRANDA

Sure I can, father.

PROSPERO

What do you remember? A house, a person? Tell me anything you remember.

MIRANDA

'Tis far off,

45 And rather like a dream than an assurance
That my remembrance warrants. Had I not
Four or five women once that tended me?

PROSPERO

Thou hadst, and more, Miranda. But how is it
That this lives in thy mind? What seest thou else
50 In the dark backward and abysm of time?
If thou rememberest aught ere thou camest here,
How thou camest here thou mayst.

MIRANDA

But that I do not.

PROSPERO

Twelve year since, Miranda, twelve year since,
Thy father was the Duke of Milan and
55 A prince of power.

MIRANDA

Sir, are not you my father?

PROSPERO

Thy mother was a piece of virtue and
She said thou wast my daughter. And thy father
Was Duke of Milan, and thou his only heir
And princess no worse issued.

MIRANDA

Oh, the heavens!
60 What foul play had we that we came from thence?
Or blessèd was 't we did?

PROSPERO

Both, both, my girl.
By foul play, as thou sayst, were we heaved thence,
But blessedly holp hither.

MIRANDA

My memory is hazy, more like a dream than a recollection. Didn't I use to have four or five women taking care of me?

PROSPERO

Indeed you did, and more besides, Miranda. But how is it possible that you still remember this, through all the darkness of the past? If you remember your life before you came here, you may also remember how you got here.

MIRANDA

No, that I don't remember.

PROSPERO

Twelve years ago, Miranda, twelve years ago your father was the Duke of Milan, a powerful prince.

MIRANDA

Aren't you my father?

PROSPERO

Your mother was extremely virtuous, and she said you were my daughter. And your father was Duke of Milan, and you were his heir, a princess.

MIRANDA

Good lord! What evil things were done to us that we were driven here? Or was it a blessing that we came here?

PROSPERO

Both, both, my girl. We were pushed out of power by evil deeds, as you call them. But we were blessed in being helped toward this island.

MIRANDA
                                        Oh, my heart bleeds
To think o' th' teen that I have turned you to,
Which is from my remembrance! Please you, farther.

PROSPERO
My brother and thy uncle, called Antonio—
I pray thee, mark me (that a brother should
Be so perfidious!)—he whom next thyself
Of all the world I loved and to him put
The manage of my state, as at that time
Through all the signories it was the first,
And Prospero the prime duke, being so reputed
In dignity, and for the liberal arts
Without a parallel. Those being all my study,
The government I cast upon my brother
And to my state grew stranger, being transported
And rapt in secret studies. Thy false uncle—
Dost thou attend me?

MIRANDA
                                    Sir, most heedfully.

PROSPERO
Being once perfected how to grant suits,
How to deny them, who t' advance and who
To trash for overtopping, new created
The creatures that were mine, I say—or changed 'em,
Or else new formed 'em—having both the key
Of officer and office, set all hearts i' th' state
To what tune pleased his ear, that now he was
The ivy which had hid my princely trunk,
And sucked my verdure out on 't. Thou attend'st not.

MIRANDA
O, good sir, I do.

MIRANDA

Oh, it breaks my heart to think how painful it must be for you to recall all this, things that I can't remember. But please tell me more.

PROSPERO

My brother, your uncle Antonio—just listen to this (I still can't believe a brother could be so disloyal!)—My brother whom—aside from you—I loved more than anyone else in the world, I trusted to run my state, which at that time was the strongest in the land, and Prospero the number one duke, famous for my dignity and my education. Since I was so drawn to studying things like logic, grammar, geometry, and astronomy, I let my control of the government slide a bit, being too wrapped up in my occult books. Your disloyal uncle—are you paying attention?

MIRANDA

I'm hanging on every word.

PROSPERO

Once Antonio got the knack of granting certain requests, denying others, promoting some officials and keeping down those who were getting too ambitious, he won over the people who used to be mine, or changed them—remade them, you might say. Since he had control over the whole government and everyone in it, he soon made everyone sing his own song—whichever song he happened to like. He became like the ivy that sticks to the side of the tree, and sucked my vitality out of me.—You're not paying attention.

MIRANDA

Oh, yes I am, father.

PROSPERO

I pray thee, mark me.

I, thus neglecting worldly ends, all dedicated
90 To closeness and the bettering of my mind
With that which, but by being so retired,
O'erprized all popular rate, in my false brother
Awaked an evil nature. And my trust,
Like a good parent, did beget of him
95 A falsehood in its contrary as great
As my trust was, which had indeed no limit,
A confidence sans bound. He being thus lorded,
Not only with what my revenue yielded
But what my power might else exact, like one
100 Who having into truth, by telling of it,
Made such a sinner of his memory
To credit his own lie—he did believe
He was indeed the duke, out o' th' substitution
And executing th' outward face of royalty,
105 With all prerogative. Hence his ambition growing—
Dost thou hear?

MIRANDA

Your tale, sir, would cure deafness.

PROSPERO

To have no screen between this part he played
And him he played it for, he needs will be
Absolute Milan. Me, poor man, my library
110 Was dukedom large enough. Of temporal royalties
He thinks me now incapable, confederates—
So dry he was for sway—wi' th' King of Naples
To give him annual tribute, do him homage,
Subject his coronet to his crown and bend
115 The dukedom yet unbowed—alas, poor Milan!—
To most ignoble stooping.

MIRANDA

Oh, the heavens!

PROSPERO

Please listen to me carefully. As I neglected practical matters, being totally dedicated to solitude and to improving my mind with subjects more valuable than most people imagine, I was so shut away from the world that I unwittingly stirred up evil wishes in my disloyal brother. My deep trust in him made him deeply untrustworthy, arousing in him a treachery as big as my trust was—my trust which had no limit, an infinite confidence. With Antonio possessing such powers and wealth, coming not only from my income but also from his ability to take whatever my authority allowed him to take, Antonio started to believe that he was the duke, like some liar who begins to believe in his own lie. He put on the face of royalty, with all the rights that go along with it. With his ambition growing like this—do you hear what I'm saying?

MIRANDA

What you're saying could cure deafness, father. Of course I hear it.

PROSPERO

To make his political performance absolutely perfect, he simply had to become the Duke of Milan himself. My library was a large enough dukedom for me. So, now Antonio judges me incapable of carrying out my duties. He's so power-hungry that he allies himself with the King of Naples, agreeing to pay him a regular annual sum, swear subservience to him, and put the dukedom of Milan—never subservient to anyone before!—under the humiliating control of Naples.

MIRANDA

Good heavens!

PROSPERO
>Mark his condition and the event. Then tell me
>If this might be a brother.

MIRANDA
>   I should sin
>To think but nobly of my grandmother.
>120   Good wombs have borne bad sons.

PROSPERO
>   Now the condition.
>The King of Naples, being an enemy
>To me inveterate, hearkens my brother's suit,
>Which was that he, in lieu o' th' premises
>Of homage and I know not how much tribute,
>125   Should presently extirpate me and mine
>Out of the dukedom, and confer fair Milan
>With all the honors on my brother. Whereon,
>A treacherous army levied, one midnight
>Fated to th' purpose did Antonio open
>130   The gates of Milan, and, i' th' dead of darkness,
>The ministers for th' purpose hurried thence
>Me and thy crying self.

MIRANDA
>   Alack, for pity!
>I, not remembering how I cried out then,
>Will cry it o'er again. It is a hint
>135   That wrings mine eyes to 't.

PROSPERO
>   Hear a little further
>And then I'll bring thee to the present business
>Which now 's upon 's, without the which this story
>Were most impertinent.

MIRANDA
>   Wherefore did they not
>That hour destroy us?

PROSPERO

Think about that, and about what followed afterward. Then tell me if Antonio can be called a brother.

MIRANDA

It would be wrong for me to think poorly of my grandmother. Good women sometimes give birth to bad sons.

PROSPERO

Now listen to the agreement they made. The king of Naples, my arch-enemy, listens to my brother's request, which was that the king, in exchange for the respect and money paid to him, would get rid of me and make my brother Duke of Milan instead. A treacherous army was gathered, and one fateful night at midnight, Antonio opened the gates of Milan, and in the pitch black had his officers rush out me and you, my dear daughter. You were crying.

MIRANDA

How awful! I can't remember how I cried then, but I'll cry all over again. This story breaks my heart.

PROSPERO

Just listen a little more, and I'll bring you up to date about the present situation, which is the whole reason I'm telling you this story in the first place.

MIRANDA

Why didn't they just kill us that night?

PROSPERO
                              Well demanded, wench.
140   My tale provokes that question. Dear, they durst not,
      So dear the love my people bore me, nor set
      A mark so bloody on the business, but
      With colors fairer painted their foul ends.
      In few, they hurried us aboard a bark,
145   Bore us some leagues to sea, where they prepared
      A rotten carcass of a butt, not rigged,
      Nor tackle, sail, nor mast. The very rats
      Instinctively had quit it. There they hoist us
      To cry to th' sea that roared to us, to sigh
150   To th' winds whose pity, sighing back again,
      Did us but loving wrong.

MIRANDA
                              Alack, what trouble
      Was I then to you!

PROSPERO
                        Oh, a cherubim
      Thou wast that did preserve me. Thou didst smile
      Infusèd with a fortitude from heaven,
155   When I have decked the sea with drops full salt,
      Under my burthen groaned; which raised in me
      An undergoing stomach to bear up
      Against what should ensue.

MIRANDA
      How came we ashore?

PROSPERO

Good question, my girl. My story does raise that question. The answer, my dear, is that they didn't dare, because the people of Milan loved me too much. The had to disguise their bloody intentions. So, to make a long story short, they hurried us onto a ship and carried us a number of miles out to sea, where they prepared a rotten carcass of a boat, with no sails or masts or ropes, which even the rats had abandoned. They tossed us in the water to cry to the sea that roared back at us, to sigh into the winds that sighed right back at us in pity.

MIRANDA

God, what a burden on you I must have been!

PROSPERO

No, my dear, you were a little angel who kept me going. You smiled with a strength you must have gotten from heaven, while I cried salty tears into the salty sea, and groaned at our situation. Your smile sustained my spirits against whatever would come our way.

MIRANDA

How did we manage to get ashore?

PROSPERO
                              By providence divine.
160   Some food we had and some fresh water that
      A noble Neapolitan, Gonzalo,
      Out of his charity, who being then appointed
      Master of this design, did give us, with
      Rich garments, linens, stuffs, and necessaries,
165   Which since have steaded much. So, of his gentleness,
      Knowing I loved my books, he furnished me
      From mine own library with volumes that
      I prize above my dukedom.

MIRANDA
                              Would I might
      But ever see that man!

PROSPERO
                              Now I arise.
      (stands and puts on his mantle)
170   Sit still, and hear the last of our sea-sorrow.
      Here in this island we arrived, and here
      Have I, thy schoolmaster, made thee more profit
      Than other princesses can that have more time
      For vainer hours and tutors not so careful.

MIRANDA
175   Heavens thank you for 't! And now, I pray you, sir—
      For still 'tis beating in my mind—your reason
      For raising this sea storm?

PROSPERO
                              Know thus far forth:
      By accident most strange, bountiful Fortune
      (Now my dear lady) hath mine enemies
180   Brought to this shore. And by my prescience
      I find my zenith doth depend upon
      A most auspicious star, whose influence
      If now I court not but omit, my fortunes
      Will ever after droop. Here cease more questions.

PROSPERO

With God's help. We had a little food and fresh water that a nobleman from Naples, Gonzalo, had given us out of the kindness of his heart. He had been chosen to carry out the plan of putting us to sea. He also gave us clothes, linen, and other necessities that have been of great help. Knowing how much I loved my books, he gave me some books from my library that I value more than my dukedom.

MIRANDA

I wish I could see that man someday!

PROSPERO

Now I'll stand up. *(he stands and puts on his magic cloak)* Sit still and listen to the last of our sad sea adventures. We arrived here on this island, where I, acting as your teacher, have given you a better education than most princesses get, princesses who have less careful tutors, who spend their time instead on empty fun.

MIRANDA

May God thank you for it. But please, father—the question is still nagging at me—why did you conjure up this storm?

PROSPERO

You should know this: much luck is on my side, and my enemies have happened to wreck their ship on this island. As I see it, my fate hangs on this lucky event, and if I handle it wrong, I'll suffer for the rest of my life. Now, no more questions.

185   Thou art inclined to sleep. 'Tis a good dullness,
And give it way. I know thou canst not choose.

MIRANDA *sleeps*

Come away, servant, come. I am ready now.
Approach, my Ariel, come.

Enter ARIEL

ARIEL
All hail, great master! Grave sir, hail! I come
190   To answer thy best pleasure, be 't to fly,
To swim, to dive into the fire, to ride
On the curled clouds. To thy strong bidding, task
Ariel and all his quality.

PROSPERO
               Hast thou, spirit,
Performed to point the tempest that I bade thee?

ARIEL
195   To every article.
I boarded the king's ship. Now on the beak,
Now in the waist, the deck, in every cabin,
I flamed amazement. Sometime I'd divide,
And burn in many places. On the topmast,
200   The yards, and bowsprit would I flame distinctly,
Then meet and join. Jove's lightning, the precursors
O' th' dreadful thunderclaps, more momentary
And sight-outrunning were not. The fire and cracks
Of sulfurous roaring the most mighty Neptune
205   Seem to besiege and make his bold waves tremble,
Yea, his dread trident shake.

PROSPERO
             My brave spirit!
Who was so firm, so constant, that this coil
Would not infect his reason?

You look sleepy. It's a nice hazy feeling, so give in to it. I know you have no choice.

MIRANDA *falls asleep.*

Come on, servant, come. I'm ready now. Come here, Ariel.

ARIEL *enters.*

ARIEL

Humble greetings, great master! Worthy sir, greetings! Your wish is my command, whatever you want. If you want me to fly, to swim, to jump into fire, to ride the clouds in the sky, Ariel will get right to the task.

PROSPERO

Spirit, did you carry out the storm just as I ordered?

ARIEL

Down to the last detail. I boarded the king's ship, and in every corner of it, from the deck to the cabins, I made everyone astonished and terrified. Sometimes I appeared in many places at once. On the top sail and main mast I flamed in different spots, then I came together into a single flame. I flashed about faster than lightning. The fire and deafening cracks seemed to overwhelm even the god of the sea himself, making him tremble underwater.

PROSPERO

Good spirit! Who could ever be so steady and strong that a disturbance like that wouldn't make him crazy?

ARIEL

                                        Not a soul
But felt a fever of the mad and played
210   Some tricks of desperation. All but mariners
Plunged in the foaming brine and quit the vessel,
Then all afire with me. The king's son, Ferdinand,
With hair up-staring—then, like reeds, not hair—
Was the first man that leaped, cried, "Hell is empty
215   And all the devils are here."

PROSPERO

                                        Why, that's my spirit!
But was not this nigh shore?

ARIEL

                                        Close by, my master.

PROSPERO

But are they, Ariel, safe?

ARIEL

                                        Not a hair perished.
On their sustaining garments not a blemish,
But fresher than before. And, as thou badest me,
220   In troops I have dispersed them 'bout the isle.
The king's son have I landed by himself,
Whom I left cooling of the air with sighs
In an odd angle of the isle, and sitting,
His arms in this sad knot.

PROSPERO

                                        Of the king's ship,
225   The mariners, say how thou hast disposed,
And all the rest o' th' fleet.

ARIEL

                                        Safely in harbor
Is the king's ship. In the deep nook where once
Thou called'st me up at midnight to fetch dew
From the still-vexed Bermoothes, there she's hid.

ARIEL

Everyone there got a little crazy and pulled some desperate stunts. Everyone except the sailors dove into the sea, leaving behind the ship that I had set on fire. The king's son, Ferdinand, with his hair standing straight up—it looked like reeds, not hair—was the first person to jump, shouting, "Hell is empty, and all the devils are here!"

PROSPERO

Good job! But was this near the shore?

ARIEL

Very near, my master.

PROSPERO

But are they all safe, Ariel?

ARIEL

Nobody was hurt in the slightest. Even their clothes are unstained, and look fresher than before the storm. I've separated them into groups around the island, just as you ordered. I sent the king's son off by himself to a faraway nook on the island, where he's sitting now sighing, with his arms crossed like this. (*he folds his arms.*)

PROSPERO

Tell me what you did with the king's ship, the sailors, and the other ships.

ARIEL

The king's ship is safely in the harbor, hidden in that deep cove where you once summoned me to bring back dew from the stormy Bermuda islands.

230 The mariners all under hatches stowed,
Who, with a charm joined to their suffered labor,
I have left asleep. And for the rest o' th' fleet,
Which I dispersed, they all have met again
And are upon the Mediterranean float,
235 Bound sadly home for Naples,
Supposing that they saw the king's ship wracked
And his great person perish.

PROSPERO
Ariel, thy charge
Exactly is performed. But there's more work.
What is the time o' th' day?

ARIEL
Past the mid season.

PROSPERO
240 At least two glasses. The time 'twixt six and now
Must by us both be spent most preciously.

ARIEL
Is there more toil? Since thou dost give me pains,
Let me remember thee what thou hast promised,
Which is not yet performed me.

PROSPERO
How now? Moody?
245 What is 't thou canst demand?

ARIEL
My liberty.

PROSPERO
Before the time be out? No more!

ARIEL
I prithee,
Remember I have done thee worthy service,
Told thee no lies, made thee no mistakings, served
Without or grudge or grumblings. Thou didst promise
250 To bate me a full year.

The sailors are all below deck, sleeping both from their labor and from a magic spell I cast over them. As for the rest of the ships, I scattered them, and they've gathered again in the Mediterranean, sailing sadly home to Naples, believing that they witnessed the shipwreck and death of their great king.

PROSPERO

Ariel, you've done your work exactly as I ordered. But there's more work to be done. What time is it?

ARIEL

Past noon.

PROSPERO

At least two hours past. We can't waste time between now and six o'clock.

ARIEL

Is there more work to do? Since you're giving me new assignments, let me remind you what you promised me but haven't come through with yet.

PROSPERO

What? You're in a bad mood? What could you possibly ask for?

ARIEL

My freedom.

PROSPERO

Before your sentence has been completed? Don't say anything else.

ARIEL

I beg you, remember the good work I've done for you, and how I've never lied to you, never made mistakes, and never grumbled in my work. You promised to take a full year off my sentence.

PROSPERO
Dost thou forget
From what a torment I did free thee?

ARIEL
No.

PROSPERO
Thou dost, and think'st it much to tread the ooze
Of the salt deep,
255 To run upon the sharp wind of the north,
To do me business in the veins o' th' earth
When it is baked with frost.

ARIEL
I do not, sir.

PROSPERO
Thou liest, malignant thing! Hast thou forgot
The foul witch Sycorax, who with age and envy
260 Was grown into a hoop? Hast thou forgot her?

ARIEL
No, sir.

PROSPERO
Thou hast. Where was she born? Speak. Tell me.

ARIEL
Sir, in Argier.

PROSPERO
Oh, was she so? I must
Once in a month recount what thou hast been,
265 Which thou forget'st. This damned witch Sycorax,
For mischiefs manifold and sorceries terrible
To enter human hearing, from Argier,
Thou know'st, was banished. For one thing she did
They would not take her life. Is not this true?

ARIEL
270 Ay, sir.

PROSPERO

Have you forgotten the torture I freed you from?

ARIEL

No.

PROSPERO

You have forgotten, and you think it's a burden when I ask you to walk through the ocean, or run on the north wind, or do business for me underground when the earth's frozen solid.

ARIEL

No, I don't, sir.

PROSPERO

You lie, you nasty, ungrateful thing! Have you forgotten the horrid witch Sycorax, stooped over with old age and ill will? Have you forgotten her?

ARIEL

No, sir.

PROSPERO

You have. Where was she born? Speak. Tell me.

ARIEL

In Algiers, sir.

PROSPERO

Oh, was she now? I'll have to tell the story again every month, since you seem to forget it. This damned witch Sycorax was kicked out of Algiers for various witching crimes too terrible for humans to hear about. But for one reason they refused to execute her. Isn't that true?

ARIEL

Yes, sir.

PROSPERO
This blue-eyed hag was hither brought with child
And here was left by th' sailors. Thou, my slave,
As thou report'st thyself, wast then her servant.
And, for thou wast a spirit too delicate
275   To act her earthy and abhorred commands,
Refusing her grand hests, she did confine thee,
By help of her more potent ministers
And in her most unmitigable rage,
Into a cloven pine, within which rift
280   Imprisoned thou didst painfully remain
A dozen years; within which space she died
And left thee there, where thou didst vent thy groans
As fast as mill wheels strike. Then was this island—
Save for the son that she did litter here,
285   A freckled whelp hag-born—not honored with
A human shape.

ARIEL
                              Yes, Caliban, her son.

PROSPERO
Dull thing, I say so. He, that Caliban
Whom now I keep in service. Thou best know'st
What torment I did find thee in. Thy groans
290   Of ever angry bears. It was a torment
Did make wolves howl and penetrate the breasts
To lay upon the damned, which Sycorax
Could not again undo. It was mine art,
When I arrived and heard thee, that made gape
295   The pine and let thee out.

ARIEL
                              I thank thee, master.

PROSPERO
If thou more murmur'st, I will rend an oak
And peg thee in his knotty entrails till
Thou hast howled away twelve winters.

PROSPERO

A mill is a building with machinery for grinding grain into flour. If built next to a river, the machinery would be driven by a paddled wheel propelled by the river.

This sunken-eyed hag was brought here pregnant and left by the sailors. You, my slave, were her servant at the time, as you admit yourself. You were too delicate to carry out her horrible orders, and you refused. In a fit of rage she locked you up in a hollow pine tree, with the help of her powerful assistants, and left you there for twelve years. During that time she died, and you were trapped, moaning and groaning as fast as the blades of a mill wheel strike the water. At that time there were no people here. This island was not honored with a human being—except for the son that Sycorax gave birth to here, a freckled baby born of an old hag.

ARIEL

Yes, Caliban, her son.

PROSPERO

That's right, you stupid thing. Caliban, who now serves me. You know better than anyone how tortured you were when I found you. Your groans made wolves howl, and even made bears feel sorry for you. Nobody but the damned souls of hell deserves the spell that Sycorax put on you and couldn't undo. It was my magic that saved you when I arrived on the island and heard you, making the pine tree open and let you out.

ARIEL

Thank you, master.

PROSPERO

If you complain any more, I'll split an oak tree and lock you up in it till you've howled for twelve years.

ARIEL

Pardon, master.

I will be correspondent to command
300   And do my spiriting gently.

PROSPERO

Do so, and after two days
I will discharge thee.

ARIEL

That's my noble master!
What shall I do? Say, what? What shall I do?

PROSPERO

Go make thyself like a nymph o' th' sea. Be subject
To no sight but thine and mine, invisible
305   To every eyeball else. Go take this shape
And hither come in 't. Go hence with diligence.

Exit ARIEL

(to MIRANDA*)*
Awake, dear heart, awake! Thou hast slept well.
Awake!

MIRANDA

(waking) The strangeness of your story put
Heaviness in me.

PROSPERO

Shake it off. Come on.
310   We'll visit Caliban, my slave who never
Yields us kind answer.

MIRANDA

'Tis a villain, sir,
I do not love to look on.

ARIEL

Please forgive me, master. I'll be obedient and do all my tasks without complaining.

PROSPERO

Do that, and I'll set you free in two days.

ARIEL

That's noble of you, master. What shall I do for you? Just tell me. What shall I do?

PROSPERO

Prospero hands Ariel a garment that makes him invisible. For the rest of the play, when we see him in the garment, we know he's invisible.

Go disguise yourself as a sea nymph. Be invisible to everyone except yourself and me. Take this garment, put it on, and then come back here. Hurry, go!

ARIEL exits.

(to MIRANDA*)* Wake up, my dear. Wake up. You've slept well. Wake up.

MIRANDA

(waking up) Your strange story made me groggy.

PROSPERO

Shake off your sleepiness. Come on. We'll go visit Caliban, my slave who always talks to us so nastily.

MIRANDA

He's an evil one, father. I don't like him.

PROSPERO
                              But as 'tis,
We cannot miss him. He does make our fire,
Fetch in our wood, and serves in offices
That profit us.—What, ho! Slave! Caliban!
Thou earth, thou! Speak.

CALIBAN
        (within)   There's wood enough within.

PROSPERO
Come forth, I say! There's other business for thee.
Come, thou tortoise! When?

Enter ARIEL, *like a water nymph*

Fine apparition! My quaint Ariel,
Hark in thine ear. *(whispers to* ARIEL)

ARIEL
                        My lord it shall be done.

Exit ARIEL

PROSPERO
        (to CALIBAN) Thou poisonous slave, got by the devil himself
Upon thy wicked dam, come forth!

Enter CALIBAN

CALIBAN
As wicked dew as e'er my mother brushed
With raven's feather from unwholesome fen
Drop on you both! A southwest blow on ye
And blister you all o'er!

315
320
325

PROSPERO

> But even so, we can't do without him. He builds our fires, gets our firewood, and does all kinds of useful things for us.—Hey! Caliban! Pile of dirt! Say something.

CALIBAN

> *(offstage)* You've got enough firewood already.

PROSPERO

> Come out, I order you. There's other work for you to do. Come on, you turtle!

> ARIEL *enters disguised as a water nymph.*

> What a fine sight! My dear clever Ariel, listen carefully. *(he whispers to* ARIEL*)*

ARIEL

> My lord, I'll do it right away.

> ARIEL *exits.*

PROSPERO

> *(to* CALIBAN*)* You horrible slave, with a wicked hag for a mother and the devil himself for a father, come out!

> CALIBAN *enters.*

CALIBAN

> I hope you both get drenched with a dew as evil as what my mother used to collect with a crow's feather from the poison swamps. May a hot southwest wind blow on you and cover you with blisters all over.

PROSPERO

For this, be sure, tonight thou shalt have cramps,
Side-stitches that shall pen thy breath up. Urchins
Shall, forth at vast of night that they may work,
All exercise on thee. Thou shalt be pinched
As thick as honeycomb, each pinch more stinging
Than bees that made 'em.

CALIBAN

I must eat my dinner.
This island's mine, by Sycorax my mother,
Which thou takest from me. When thou camest first,
Thou strok'st me and made much of me, wouldst give me
Water with berries in 't, and teach me how
To name the bigger light, and how the less,
That burn by day and night. And then I loved thee
And showed thee all the qualities o' th' isle,
The fresh springs, brine pits, barren place and fertile.
Cursed be I that did so! All the charms
Of Sycorax, toads, beetles, bats, light on you!
For I am all the subjects that you have,
Which first was mine own king. And here you sty me
In this hard rock, whiles you do keep from me
The rest o' th' island.

PROSPERO

Thou most lying slave,
Whom stripes may move, not kindness! I have used thee,
Filth as thou art, with human care, and lodged thee
In mine own cell till thou didst seek to violate
The honor of my child.

CALIBAN

Oh ho, oh ho! Would 't had been done!
Thou didst prevent me. I had peopled else
This isle with Calibans.

PROSPERO

> I'll give you cramps for saying that—horrible pains in your sides that will keep you from breathing. I'll send goblins out at night to work their nasty deeds on you. You'll be pricked all over, and it'll sting like bees.

CALIBAN

> I have to eat my dinner now. This island belongs to me because Sycorax, my mother, left it to me. But you've taken it from me. When you first got here, you petted me and took care of me, you would give me water with berries in it, and you taught me the names for the sun and the moon, the big light and the smaller light that burn in daytime and nighttime. I loved you back then. I showed you all the features of the island, the freshwater springs, the saltwater pits, the barren places and the fertile ones. I curse myself for doing that! I wish I could use all the magic spells of Sycorax against you and plague you with toads, beetles, and bats. I'm the only subject you have in your kingdom, and you were my first king, and you pen me up in this cave and don't let me go anywhere else on the island.

PROSPERO

> You liar, you respond better to the whip than to kindness! I took good care of you—piece of filth that you are—and let you stay in my own hut until you tried to rape my daughter.

CALIBAN

> Oh ho, oh ho! I wish I had! You stopped me. If you hadn't, I would have filled this island with a race of Calibans.

MIRANDA

                       Abhorrèd slave,
Which any print of goodness wilt not take,
355   Being capable of all ill! I pitied thee,
Took pains to make thee speak, taught thee each hour
One thing or other. When thou didst not, savage,
Know thine own meaning, but wouldst gabble like
A thing most brutish, I endowed thy purposes
360   With words that made them known. But thy vile race,
Though thou didst learn, had that in 't which good natures
Could not abide to be with. Therefore wast thou
Deservedly confined into this rock,
Who hadst deserved more than a prison.

CALIBAN

365   You taught me language, and my profit on 't
Is I know how to curse. The red plague rid you
For learning me your language!

PROSPERO

                       Hag-seed, hence!
Fetch us in fuel. And be quick, thou 'rt best,
To answer other business. Shrug'st thou, malice?
370   If thou neglect'st or dost unwillingly
What I command, I'll rack thee with old cramps,
Fill all thy bones with aches, make thee roar
That beasts shall tremble at thy din.

CALIBAN

                       No, pray thee.
(aside) I must obey. His art is of such power,
375   It would control my dam's god, Setebos,
And make a vassal of him.

PROSPERO

                 So, slave, hence!

Exit CALIBAN

MIRANDA

You horrid slave, you can't be trained to be good, and you're capable of anything evil! I pitied you, worked hard to teach you to speak, and taught you some new thing practically every hour. When you didn't know what you were saying, and were babbling like an animal, I helped you find words to make your point understandable. But you had bad blood in you, no matter how much you learned, and good people couldn't stand to be near you. So you got what you deserved, and were locked up in this cave, which is more fitting for the likes of you than a prison would be.

CALIBAN

You taught me language, and all I can do with it is curse. Damn you for teaching me your language!

PROSPERO

Get out of here, you son of a bitch! Bring us wood, and be quick about it. Are you shrugging and making faces, you evil thing? If you neglect my orders or do them grudgingly, I'll double you up with pains and cramps, and make all your bones ache, and make you scream so loud that the wild animals will tremble when they hear you.

CALIBAN

No, please. *(to himself)* I have to obey. He's got such strong magic powers that he could conquer and enslave the god, Setebos, that my mother used to worship.

PROSPERO

Go then, slave.

CALIBAN *exits.*

Enter FERDINAND *and* ARIEL, *invisible, playing and singing*

ARIEL
            (sings)
                        Come unto these yellow sands,
                        And then take hands.
                        Curtsied when you have, and kissed
380   The wild waves whist.
                        Foot it featly here and there,
                        And, sweet sprites, bear
                        The burden. Hark, hark!

SPIRITS
            (dispersedly, within) Bow-wow.

ARIEL
385   The watchdogs bark.

SPIRITS
            (within) Bow-wow.

ARIEL
            Hark, hark! I hear
            The strain of strutting chanticleer
            Cry "Cock-a-diddle-dow."

FERDINAND
390   Where should this music be? I' th' air or th' earth?
            It sounds no more, and sure, it waits upon
            Some god o' th' island. Sitting on a bank,
            Weeping again the king my father's wrack,
            This music crept by me upon the waters,
395   Allaying both their fury and my passion
            With its sweet air. Thence I have followed it,
            Or it hath drawn me rather. But 'tis gone.
            No, it begins again.

FERDINAND *enters with* ARIEL, *who is invisible and playing music and singing.*

ARIEL

(*singing*)
> Come onto these yellow sands,
> And we'll join hands,
> When you've curtsied and kissed
> The waves into silence.
> Prance lightly here and there,
> And the sweet spirits bear
> The burden. Listen, listen!

SPIRITS

(*refrain of the song is heard offstage, from different places, not in unison*) Bow-wow.

ARIEL

The watchdogs bark.

SPIRITS

(*offstage*) Bow-wow.

ARIEL

Listen, listen! I hear
The tune of the strutting rooster
Who cries cock-a-doodle-doo.

FERDINAND

Where's that music coming from? From the earth, or the air? It's stopped now—it must be played for some local god of the island. As I sat on the shore crying over my father's shipwreck, I heard the music creep over the wild waves, calming their fury and soothing my own grief with its sweet melodies. I followed it here, or I should say it dragged me here. But now it's stopped. No, there it is again.

ARIEL
(sings)
> Full fathom five thy father lies.
400 > Of his bones are coral made.
> Those are pearls that were his eyes.
> Nothing of him that doth fade,
> But doth suffer a sea-change
> Into something rich and strange.
405 > Sea-nymphs hourly ring his knell

SPIRITS
(within) Ding-dong.

ARIEL
Hark, now I hear them.

SPIRITS
(within)   Ding-dong, bell.

FERDINAND
The ditty does remember my drowned father.
This is no mortal business, nor no sound
410 That the earth owes. I hear it now above me.

PROSPERO
(to MIRANDA) The fringèd curtains of thine eye advance
And say what thou seest yond.

MIRANDA
                              What is 't? A spirit?
Lord, how it looks about! Believe me, sir,
It carries a brave form. But 'tis a spirit.

PROSPERO
415 No, wench! It eats and sleeps and hath such senses
As we have, such. This gallant which thou seest
Was in the wrack. And, but he's something stained
With grief that's beauty's canker, thou mightst call him
A goodly person. He hath lost his fellows
420 And strays about to find 'em.

ARIEL

(singing)

1 fathom = 6 feet

> *Your father lies five whole fathoms below,*
> *His bones have turned to coral now.*
> *His eyes have turned to pearls.*
> *There's nothing left of him,*
> *He's undergone a complete sea change*
> *And become something rich and strange.*
> *Sea nymphs ring his death bell every hour.*

SPIRITS

(refrain, offstage) Ding-dong.

ARIEL

Listen, I hear them.

SPIRITS

Ding dong, bell.

FERDINAND

This song's about my dead father. It couldn't be sung by mere mortals. I hear it now overhead.

PROSPERO

(to MIRANDA*)* Raise the curtains of your eyelids and go take a peek at what you can see out there.

MIRANDA

What is it? A spirit? Lord, it's glancing every which way! How handsome it is. It must be a spirit.

PROSPERO

No, girl! It eats and sleeps and has the same five senses we do. The gentleman you see now was in the shipwreck, and if he weren't a little spoiled by grief, which always ruins good looks, you could call him handsome. He's lost his comrades and is wandering around looking for them.

MIRANDA

                              I might call him
A thing divine, for nothing natural
I ever saw so noble.

PROSPERO

(aside)   It goes on, I see,
As my soul prompts it.—Spirit, fine spirit! I'll free thee
Within two days for this.

FERDINAND

(seeing MIRANDA*)*   Most sure, the goddess
425 On whom these airs attend!—Vouchsafe my prayer
May know if you remain upon this island,
And that you will some good instruction give
How I may bear me here. My prime request,
Which I do last pronounce, is—O you wonder!—
430 If you be maid or no.

MIRANDA

                              No wonder, sir,
But certainly a maid.

FERDINAND

                              My language! Heavens,
I am the best of them that speak this speech,
Were I but where 'tis spoken.

PROSPERO

                              How? The best?
What wert thou if the King of Naples heard thee?

FERDINAND

435 A single thing, as I am now, that wonders
To hear thee speak of Naples. He does hear me,
And that he does I weep. Myself am Naples,
Who with mine eyes, never since at ebb, beheld
The king my father wracked.

MIRANDA

                              Alack, for mercy!

MIRANDA

> I could imagine he's divine, since I never saw anything so noble-looking on earth before.

PROSPERO

> *(to himself)* It's all happening according to plan, just as my soul wanted it to happen. *(to* ARIEL*)* Spirit, you fine spirit, I'll set you free in two days for doing such a good job here.

FERDINAND

> *(seeing* MIRANDA*)* This must surely be the goddess that the music is being played for!—Please, I beg you to answer me, tell me if you live on this island, and tell me how I should behave here. My main question, which I save for the last, is—Oh, you marvelous creature!—are you a maiden or a goddess?

MIRANDA

> I'm not marvelous, sir, but I'm certainly a maiden.

FERDINAND

> She speaks my language! My God, I'm the highest-ranking person who speaks this language—if only we were back where it's spoken.

PROSPERO

> What's that? The highest-ranking? What would the King of Naples do if he heard you say that?

FERDINAND

> He would just see me for what I am, a person amazed to hear you talking about Naples. He does hear me, and that makes me cry. I myself am the King of Naples, since I saw with my own eyes—these eyes that haven't been dry since—my father killed in a shipwreck.

MIRANDA

> Ah, how pitiful!

FERDINAND

440   Yes, faith, and all his lords, the Duke of Milan
And his brave son being twain.

PROSPERO

(aside)   The Duke of Milan
And his more braver daughter could control thee
If now 'twere fit to do 't! At the first sight
They have changed eyes.—Delicate Ariel,
445   I'll set thee free for this.

(to FERDINAND)

A word, good sir.
I fear you have done yourself some wrong. A word.

MIRANDA

(aside) Why speaks my father so ungently? This
Is the third man that e'er I saw, the first
That e'er I sighed for. Pity move my father
450   To be inclined my way!

FERDINAND

(to MIRANDA)

Oh, if a virgin,
And your affection not gone forth, I'll make you
The queen of Naples.

PROSPERO

Soft, sir! One word more.

(aside)

They are both in either's powers, but this swift business
455   I must uneasy make lest too light winning
Make the prize light.

(to FERDINAND)

One word more. I charge thee
That thou attend me. Thou dost here usurp
The name thou owest not, and hast put thyself
Upon this island as a spy to win it
460   From me, the lord on 't.

FERDINAND

No, as I am a man!

FERDINAND

Yes, indeed, and all the King's men, the Duke of Milan and his fine son too.

PROSPERO

(to himself) The real Duke of Milan and his far finer daughter could beat you in a heartbeat, if it were the right time. They've fallen in love at first sight!—Wonderful Ariel, I'll set you free for doing such good work here. *(to* **FERDINAND***)* Could I have a word with you, sir? I'm afraid you've made a mistake. Just a word.

MIRANDA

(to herself) Why is my father speaking to him so rudely? This is the third man I've ever seen in my life, and the first one I've felt romantic feelings for. I hope my father takes pity on me and treats him well for my sake!

FERDINAND

Oh, if you're a virgin, and you haven't given your heart to another man, then I'll make you the queen of Naples.

PROSPERO

Hang on, sir! Just a moment. *(to himself)* They're both in love. But I need to cause a little trouble between them, or else they'll never appreciate the value of their love. *(to* **FERDINAND***)* I need a word with you, sir. I order you to listen to me. You're calling yourself by a name that doesn't belong to you. You've come onto this island as a spy, to snatch it away from me—I'm the rightful lord of it.

FERDINAND

No, I swear, that's not true!

MIRANDA
>There's nothing ill can dwell in such a temple.
>If the ill spirit have so fair a house,
>Good things will strive to dwell with 't.

PROSPERO
>(*to* FERDINAND)   Follow me.
465 (*to* MIRANDA) Speak not you for him. He's a traitor.
>(*to* FERDINAND)   Come,
>I'll manacle thy neck and feet together.
>Seawater shalt thou drink. Thy food shall be
>The fresh-brook mussles, withered roots, and husks
>Wherein the acorn cradled. Follow.

FERDINAND
>   No.
470 I will resist such entertainment till
>Mine enemy has more power.

>FERDINAND *draws his sword, and is charmed from moving*

MIRANDA
>   O dear father,
>Make not too rash a trial of him, for
>He's gentle and not fearful.

PROSPERO
>   What, I say?
>My foot my tutor?—Put thy sword up, traitor,
475 Who makest a show but darest not strike, thy conscience
>Is so possessed with guilt. Come from thy ward,
>For I can here disarm thee with this stick
>And make thy weapon drop.

MIRANDA
>   Beseech you, father.

PROSPERO
>Hence! Hang not on my garments.

MIRANDA

A man as handsome as that can't have anything evil in him. If the devil had such a beautiful house as his body, then good things would fight to live in it.

PROSPERO

(to FERDINAND*)* Follow me. *(to* MIRANDA*)* Don't defend him. He's a traitor. *(to* FERDINAND*)* Come on, I'll chain your neck and feet together, and I'll give you sea water to drink. Your food will be slugs, dry roots, and acorn shells. Come on.

FERDINAND

No, I'll have to decline that offer—at least as long as I'm stronger than you are.

FERDINAND *takes out his sword, but* PROSPERO *casts a spell on him that freezes him in place.*

MIRANDA

Oh, dear father, don't judge him too quickly. He's a good man, and brave too.

PROSPERO

What's that? The daughter knows more than the father?—Put away your sword, traitor. You make quite a show there, but you're too scared to strike at me, since you feel too guilty. Get out of that position, because I can disarm you with my magic wand and make your sword drop.

MIRANDA

Please, father, I beg you.

PROSPERO

Let go of me! Don't tug on my clothes.

MIRANDA
                                              Sir, have pity,
480   I'll be his surety.

PROSPERO
                                    Silence! One word more
        Shall make me chide thee, if not hate thee. What,
        An advocate for an imposter? Hush,
        Thou think'st there is no more such shapes as he,
        Having seen but him and Caliban. Foolish wench,
485   To th' most of men this is a Caliban
        And they to him are angels.

MIRANDA
                                              My affections
        Are then most humble. I have no ambition
        To see a goodlier man.

PROSPERO
        (to FERDINAND*)*   Come on. Obey.
        Thy nerves are in their infancy again
490   And have no vigor in them.

FERDINAND
                                        So they are.
        My spirits, as in a dream, are all bound up.
        My father's loss, the weakness which I feel,
        The wrack of all my friends, nor this man's threats,
        To whom I am subdued, are but light to me,
495   Might I but through my prison once a day
        Behold this maid. All corners else o' th' earth
        Let liberty make use of. Space enough
        Have I in such a prison.

PROSPERO
        (aside)   It works!
        (to FERDINAND*)*   Come on.
        (aside) Thou hast done well, fine Ariel!
        (to FERDINAND*)*   Follow me.
500   *(to* ARIEL*)* Hark what thou else shalt do me.

MIRANDA

Father, take pity on him. I'll guarantee his goodness myself.

PROSPERO

Quiet! If you say one more word, I'll punish you, maybe even hate you. You're defending an impostor? Be quiet. You think he's special, since you've only ever seen him and Caliban. Foolish girl, in the eyes of most people this man's a Caliban, and compared to him, they're angels.

MIRANDA

Then my love is humble. I don't feel any urge to see a more handsome man than this one.

PROSPERO

(to FERDINAND*)* Come on. Obey my orders. Your muscles are all limp and lifeless.

FERDINAND

That's true, they are. My strength is all gone, as if in a dream. The death of my father, my physical weakness, the loss of all my friends, the threats of this man who's taken me prisoner—all that would be easy for me to take, if only I could look through my prison windows once a day and see this girl. I don't need any more freedom than that. A prison like that would give me enough liberty.

PROSPERO

(to himself) It's working! *(to* FERDINAND*)* Come on. *(to himself)* You've done well, Ariel. *(to* FERDINAND*)* Follow me. *(to* ARIEL*)* Listen to what you'll do for me next.

MIRANDA
500   *(to* **FERDINAND***)*   Be of comfort.
         My father's of a better nature, sir,
         Than he appears by speech. This is unwonted
         Which now came from him.

PROSPERO
         (to **ARIEL***)*   Thou shalt be free
         As mountain winds. But then exactly do
505   All points of my command.

ARIEL
         To th' syllable.

PROSPERO
         (to **FERDINAND***)* Come, follow.
         (to **MIRANDA***)*—Speak not for him.

                                              Exeunt

MIRANDA

> *(to FERDINAND)* Don't worry, my father's kinder than his words just now make him sound. What he said didn't sound like him at all.

PROSPERO

> *(to ARIEL)* You'll be free as a bird. But you have to do exactly what I order.

ARIEL

> Down to the last detail.

PROSPERO

> *(to FERDINAND)* Come, follow me. *(to MIRANDA)* Don't defend him.

> *They exit.*

ACT TWO
SCENE 1

Enter ALONSO, SEBASTIAN, ANTONIO, GONZALO, ADRIAN, FRANCISCO, *and others*

GONZALO
(to ALONSO*)* Beseech you, sir, be merry. You have cause,
So have we all, of joy, for our escape
Is much beyond our loss. Our hint of woe
Is common. Every day some sailor's wife,
5   The masters of some merchant, and the merchant
Have just our theme of woe. But for the miracle—
I mean our preservation—few in millions
Can speak like us. Then wisely, good sir, weigh
Our sorrow with our comfort.

ALONSO
                    Prithee, peace.

SEBASTIAN
10   *(to* ANTONIO*)* He receives comfort like cold porridge.

ANTONIO
(to SEBASTIAN*)* The visitor will not give him o'er so.

SEBASTIAN
Look he's winding up the watch of his wit. By and by it will strike.

GONZALO
(to ALONSO*)* Sir—

SEBASTIAN
15   *(to* ANTONIO*)* One. Tell.

GONZALO
When every grief is entertained that's offered,
Comes to th' entertainer—

ACT TWO

SCENE 1

ALONSO, SEBASTIAN, ANTONIO, GONZALO, ADRIAN, FRANCISCO, *and others enter.*

GONZALO

(to ALONSO*)* Please cheer up, sir. Like all of us, you have a good reason to be happy. The fact that we're alive outweighs our losses. Many people every day feel the sadness we feel now. Every day some sailor's wife, a ship's crew, the merchant who hired the ship all experience the same loss we've undergone. But the miracle—the fact that we were saved—only happens to a few people out of millions. So remember that, and take comfort in it, to counterbalance our sadness.

ALONSO

Please say no more.

SEBASTIAN

(to ANTONIO*)* Alonso enjoys these comforting words about as much as cold oatmeal.

ANTONIO

(to SEBASTIAN*)* But the goodwill ambassador won't give up that easily.

SEBASTIAN

(to ANTONIO*)* Look. He's like a clock winding up to strike the hour.

GONZALO

(to ALONSO*)* Sir—

SEBASTIAN

(to ANTONIO*)* There he goes! Now we can tell what time it is.

GONZALO

If we let every sad thing that happens to us get us down, then we would find ourselves—

SEBASTIAN
A dollar.

GONZALO
Dolor comes to him, indeed. You have spoken truer than
20   you purposed.

SEBASTIAN
You have taken it wiselier than I meant you should.

GONZALO
(to ALONSO*)* Therefore, my lord—

ANTONIO
(to SEBASTIAN*)* Fie, what a spendthrift is he of his tongue!

ALONSO
(to GONZALO*)* I prithee, spare.

GONZALO
25   Well, I have done. But yet—

SEBASTIAN
(to ANTONIO*)* He will be talking.

ANTONIO
Which, of he or Adrian, for a good wager, first begins to
crow?

SEBASTIAN
The old cock.

ANTONIO
30   The cockerel.

SEBASTIAN
Done. The wager?

ANTONIO
A laughter.

SEBASTIAN
A match!

ADRIAN
Though this island seem to be desert—

ANTONIO
35   *(to* SEBASTIAN*)* Ha, ha, ha!

SEBASTIAN

What a pain.

GONZALO

Pain, yes indeed. We would find ourselves in pain. You thought you were being funny, but you said the truth.

SEBASTIAN

You're taking it more seriously than I meant it.

GONZALO

(to ALONSO*)* Therefore, sir—

ANTONIO

(to SEBASTIAN*)* God, doesn't he ever shut up?

ALONSO

(to GONZALO*)* Please, no more.

GONZALO

Well, I'm nearly finished. But just one last thing—

SEBASTIAN

(to ANTONIO*)* He insists on talking.

ANTONIO

Hey, let's bet. Which one will start yammering first, Gonzalo or Adrian?

SEBASTIAN

The old guy.

ANTONIO

I pick the younger one.

SEBASTIAN

You're on. What's the prize?

ANTONIO

A good laugh.

SEBASTIAN

It's a deal!

ADRIAN

Though this island may appear desolate—

ANTONIO

(to SEBASTIAN*)* Ha, ha, ha!

SEBASTIAN
So you're paid.

ADRIAN
Uninhabitable and almost inaccessible—

SEBASTIAN
Yet—

ADRIAN
Yet—

ANTONIO
40 He could not miss 't.

ADRIAN
It must needs be of subtle, tender, and delicate temperance.

ANTONIO
Temperance was a delicate wench.

SEBASTIAN
Ay, and a subtle, as he most learnedly delivered.

ADRIAN
The air breathes upon us here most sweetly.

SEBASTIAN
45 As if it had lungs, and rotten ones.

ANTONIO
Or as 'twere perfumed by a fen.

GONZALO
Here is everything advantageous to life.

ANTONIO
True. Save means to live.

SEBASTIAN
Of that there's none, or little.

GONZALO
50 How lush and lusty the grass looks! How green!

ANTONIO
The ground indeed is tawny.

SEBASTIAN
With an eye of green in 't.

ANTONIO
He misses not much.

SEBASTIAN

Fine, you win.

ADRIAN

Uninhabitable and almost inaccessible, as it were—

SEBASTIAN

Now he's going to say "but"—

ADRIAN

But—

ANTONIO

He had to say it, it was unavoidable.

ADRIAN

The island must be mild, and have a temperate climate.

ANTONIO

I knew Temperance—she was a fine girl.

SEBASTIAN

Yes, and she was mild too.

ADRIAN

There's always a breath of fresh air here.

SEBASTIAN

A breath from rotten lungs, maybe.

ANTONIO

Stinking like a swamp.

GONZALO

This island contains everything beneficial to life.

ANTONIO

True. Everything except something to live on.

SEBASTIAN

There's little or nothing of that.

GONZALO

Look how lush and healthy the grass is! How green!

ANTONIO

The ground is brown.

SEBASTIAN

With a touch of green in it.

ANTONIO

He doesn't miss a thing.

SEBASTIAN
No, he doth but mistake the truth totally.

GONZALO
55   But the rarity of it is—which is indeed almost beyond
credit—

SEBASTIAN
As many vouched rarities are.

GONZALO
That our garments, being, as they were, drenched in the
sea, hold notwithstanding their freshness and glosses,
60   being rather new-dyed than stained with salt water.

ANTONIO
If but one of his pockets could speak, would it not say he
lies?

SEBASTIAN
Ay, or very falsely pocket up his report.

GONZALO
Methinks our garments are now as fresh as when we put
65   them on first in Afric, at the marriage of the king's fair
daughter Claribel to the King of Tunis.

SEBASTIAN
'Twas a sweet marriage, and we prosper well in our return.

ADRIAN
Tunis was never graced before with such a paragon to their
queen.

GONZALO
70   Not since widow Dido's time.

ANTONIO
Widow! A pox o' that! How came that "widow" in? Widow
Dido!

SEBASTIAN

No, he just gets reality completely wrong.

GONZALO

But the really unbelievable thing is—and this is incredible—

SEBASTIAN

As most unbelievable things are.

GONZALO

That our clothes were drenched with sea water, but they came out looking brand-new.

ANTONIO

Listen to him. If his clothes could talk, they'd call him a liar.

SEBASTIAN

Or stuff what he says into their pockets.

GONZALO

Seriously, I think our clothes are as fresh now as they were the day we put them on in Africa, when we attended the marriage of the king's daughter Claribel to the King of Tunis.

SEBASTIAN

It was a lovely wedding, and we're doing really well on our trip home.

ADRIAN

Tunis has never had such a beautiful queen.

GONZALO

Not since the days of widow Dido.

According to Greek legend, Dido was the founder of the city of Carthage, on the coast of Africa.

ANTONIO

Widow? Why the hell is he calling her "widow Dido"?

SEBASTIAN

    What if he had said "widower Æneas" too? Good Lord,
how you take it!

ADRIAN

75   "Widow Dido" said you? You make me study of that. She
was of Carthage, not of Tunis.

GONZALO

    This Tunis, sir, was Carthage.

ADRIAN

    Carthage?

GONZALO

    I assure you, Carthage.

SEBASTIAN

80   His word is more than the miraculous harp. He hath raised
the wall and houses too.

ANTONIO

    What impossible matter will he make easy next?

SEBASTIAN

    I think he will carry this island home in his pocket and give
it his son for an apple.

ANTONIO

85   And sowing the kernels of it in the sea, bring forth more
islands.

GONZALO

    Ay.

ANTONIO

    Why, in good time.

GONZALO

    (to ALONSO*)* Sir, we were talking that our garments seem
90   now as fresh as when we were at Tunis at the marriage of
your daughter, who is now queen.

SEBASTIAN

Next thing you know, he'll be saying "widower Aeneas."

ADRIAN

"Widow Dido," did you say? I'm not sure about that. Dido was from Carthage, not Tunis.

GONZALO

Tunis *was* Carthage, sir.

Gonzalo is mistaken in identifying Carthage with Tunis.

ADRIAN

Carthage?

GONZALO

I'm telling you, it was Carthage.

SEBASTIAN

Gonzalo is a miracle-worker. If he says Carthage was here, then Carthage must be here.

ANTONIO

What miracle will he work next?

SEBASTIAN

I think he'll carry this island home in his pocket and give it to his son like an apple.

ANTONIO

And then throw the seeds in the sea, to make more islands grow.

GONZALO

Yes indeed.

ANTONIO

Absolutely, yes indeed.

GONZALO

(to ALONSO) Sir, we were saying that our clothes seem just as fresh as they did when we attended the wedding of your daughter, who's now queen of Tunis.

ANTONIO
> And the rarest that e'er came there.

SEBASTIAN
> Bate, I beseech you, widow Dido.

ANTONIO
> Oh, widow Dido? Ay, widow Dido.

GONZALO
95
> Is not, sir, my doublet as fresh as the first day I wore it? I
> mean, in a sort.

ANTONIO
> That "sort" was well fished for.

GONZALO
> When I wore it at your daughter's marriage?

ALONSO
> You cram these words into mine ears against
100
> The stomach of my sense. Would I had never
> Married my daughter there! For, coming thence,
> My son is lost and, in my rate, she too,
> Who is so far from Italy removed
> I ne'er again shall see her.—O thou mine heir
105
> Of Naples and of Milan, what strange fish
> Hath made his meal on thee?

FRANCISCO
>   Sir, he may live.
> I saw him beat the surges under him,
> And ride upon their backs. He trod the water,
> Whose enmity he flung aside, and breasted
110
> The surge most swoll'n that met him. His bold head
> 'Bove the contentious waves he kept, and oared
> Himself with his good arms in lusty stroke
> To th' shore, that o'er his wave-worn basis bowed,
> As stooping to relieve him. I not doubt
115
> He came alive to land.

ANTONIO

The most beautiful queen they ever had.

SEBASTIAN

I beg your pardon, except for the widow Dido.

ANTONIO

Oh, except for the widow Dido? That's right, except for the widow Dido.

GONZALO

Isn't my vest just as clean and fresh as the day I put it on? In a way, I mean.

ANTONIO

"In a way" is the right way to go.

GONZALO

I mean when I wore it at your daughter's wedding.

ALONSO

You keep cramming words into my ears that I don't want to hear. I wish that wedding had never happened, since I lost my son because of it, and I lost my daughter too in a way, since she's moved so far from Milan that I'll never see her again.—Oh, dear son of mine and heir of Naples and Milan, what strange fish has made a meal of you?

FRANCISCO

Sir, he may still be alive. I saw him swimming strongly, almost as if he was riding the waves. He treaded water and kept his head well above the wild waters coming at him, swimming with his strong arms toward the shore, which almost seemed eager to welcome him. I have no doubt he got ashore alive.

ALONSO

No, no, he's gone.

SEBASTIAN

Sir, you may thank yourself for this great loss,
That would not bless our Europe with your daughter,
But rather loose her to an African,
Where she at least is banished from your eye,
120   Who hath cause to wet the grief on 't.

ALONSO

Prithee, peace.

SEBASTIAN

You were kneeled to and importuned otherwise
By all of us, and the fair soul herself
Weighed between loathness and obedience, at
Which end o' th' beam should bow. We have lost your son,
125   I fear, forever. Milan and Naples have
More widows in them of this business' making
Than we bring men to comfort them.
The fault's your own.

ALONSO

So is the dearest o' th' loss.

GONZALO

My lord Sebastian,
130   The truth you speak doth lack some gentleness
And time to speak it in. You rub the sore
When you should bring the plaster.

SEBASTIAN

Very well.

ANTONIO

And most chirurgeonly.

GONZALO

(to ALONSO) It is foul weather in us all, good sir,
135   When you are cloudy.

ALONSO

No, no, he's dead.

SEBASTIAN

Sir, you can thank yourself for this great loss, because you wouldn't bless Europe with your daughter, but instead pimped her out to an African. At least you can be thankful that she won't be around to remind you of your loss.

ALONSO

Please be quiet.

SEBASTIAN

We all begged you not to go ahead with those marriage plans, and your lovely daughter struggled between disgust at marrying an African and the desire to obey you. Now I'm afraid we've lost your son forever. Our shipwreck has made more women widows in Milan and Naples than there are survivors to comfort them. And it's all your fault.

ALONSO

And the greatest sorrow is mine too.

GONZALO

My lord Sebastian, even though what you say is true, your way of saying it is tactless and comes at the wrong time. You're rubbing salt in his wounds when you should be applying bandages.

SEBASTIAN

All right, I'll stop.

ANTONIO

Like a good doctor.

GONZALO

(to ALONSO*)* It's bad times for all of us, sir, when you're feeling gloomy.

SEBASTIAN
                              Foul weather?

ANTONIO
                                        Very foul.

GONZALO
          Had I plantation of this isle, my lord—

ANTONIO
          He'd sow 't with nettle seed.

SEBASTIAN
                                        Or docks, or mallows.

GONZALO
          And were the king on 't, what would I do?

SEBASTIAN
          'Scape being drunk for want of wine.

GONZALO
140   I' th' commonwealth I would by contraries
          Execute all things. For no kind of traffic
          Would I admit. No name of magistrate.
          Letters should not be known. Riches, poverty,
          And use of service—none. Contract, succession,
145   Bourn, bound of land, tilth, vineyard—none.
          No use of metal, corn, or wine, or oil.
          No occupation. All men idle, all.
          And women too, but innocent and pure.
          No sovereignty—

SEBASTIAN
                              Yet he would be king on 't.

ANTONIO
150   The latter end of his commonwealth forgets the beginning.

GONZALO
          All things in common nature should produce
          Without sweat or endeavor. Treason, felony,
          Sword, pike, knife, gun, or need of any engine,
          Would I not have. But nature should bring forth
155   Of its own kind all foison, all abundance,
          To feed my innocent people.

SEBASTIAN

Bad times?

ANTONIO

Yes, very bad.

GONZALO

If I could colonize this island, my lord—

ANTONIO

He'd cultivate weeds on it.

SEBASTIAN

Or thorn-bushes.

GONZALO

And if I were king of it, you know what I'd do?

SEBASTIAN

He wouldn't get drunk much, since there's no wine here.

GONZALO

In my kingdom I'd do everything differently from the way it's usually done. I wouldn't allow any commerce. There'd be no officials or administrators. There'd be no schooling or literature. There'd be no riches, no poverty, and no servants—none. No contracts or inheritance laws; no division of the land into private farms, no metal-working, agriculture, or vineyards. There'd be no work. Men would have nothing to do, and women also—but they'd be innocent and pure. There'd be no kingship—

SEBASTIAN

He wants to be king in a place with no kingship.

ANTONIO

Yes, he's getting a bit confused.

GONZALO

Everything would be produced without labor, and would be shared by all. There'd be no treason, crimes, or weapons. Nature would produce its harvests in abundance, to feed my innocent people.

SEBASTIAN
No marrying 'mong his subjects?

ANTONIO
None, man. All idle. Whores and knaves.

GONZALO
I would with such perfection govern, sir,
160   T' excel the Golden Age.

SEBASTIAN
                   'Save his majesty!

ANTONIO
Long live Gonzalo!

GONZALO
(to ALONSO*)*   And—do you mark me, sir?

ALONSO
Prithee, no more. Thou dost talk nothing to me.

GONZALO
I do well believe your highness, and did it to minister
occasion to these gentlemen, who are of such sensible and
165   nimble lungs that they always use to laugh at nothing.

ANTONIO
'Twas you we laughed at.

GONZALO
Who in this kind of merry fooling am nothing to you. So
you may continue and laugh at nothing still.

ANTONIO
What a blow was there given!

SEBASTIAN
170   An it had not fallen flat-long.

GONZALO
You are gentlemen of brave mettle. You would lift the moon
out of her sphere if she would continue in it five weeks
without changing.

SEBASTIAN

There'd be no marriage?

ANTONIO

No. Everyone would have nothing to do. They'd all be whores and slackers.

GONZALO

I would rule so perfectly that my country would outshine the Golden Age they had in ancient times.

SEBASTIAN

Long live his Majesty!

ANTONIO

All hail Gonzalo!

GONZALO

(to ALONSO*)* Are you listening to me, sir?

ALONSO

Oh, please be quiet. You're spouting empty words.

GONZALO

You're absolutely right, your highness. I talked like that to give these gentlemen here a chance to have a good laugh. They love to laugh at empty words.

ANTONIO

It's you we were laughing at.

GONZALO

But from your perspective I don't matter, so I'm just an empty nobody for you. Go ahead and laugh at my empty words some more.

ANTONIO

Ouch, what a comeback!

SEBASTIAN

He sure did. Too bad it fell flat.

GONZALO

You're brave gentlemen. You'd give the moon a shove if it got stuck five weeks in its orbit.

Enter ARIEL *invisible, playing solemn music*

SEBASTIAN
> We would so, and then go a-batfowling.

ANTONIO
175 *(to* GONZALO*)* Nay, good my lord, be not angry.

GONZALO
> No, I warrant you. I will not adventure my discretion so
> weakly. Will you laugh me asleep, for I am very heavy?

ANTONIO
> Go sleep, and hear us.

All sleep except ALONSO, SEBASTIAN, *and* ANTONIO

ALONSO
> What, all so soon asleep? I wish mine eyes
180 Would with themselves shut up my thoughts. I find
> They are inclined to do so.

SEBASTIAN
>   Please you, sir,
> Do not omit the heavy offer of it.
> It seldom visits sorrow. When it doth,
> It is a comforter.

ANTONIO
>   We two, my lord,
185 Will guard your person while you take your rest
> And watch your safety.

ALONSO
>   Thank you. Wondrous heavy.

(falls asleep)

>   *Exit* ARIEL

ARIEL enters, invisible, playing solemn music.

SEBASTIAN

That's right, and then after we fixed the moon, we'd go bird-hunting.

ANTONIO

(to GONZALO) Don't be angry with us, my lord.

GONZALO

I'm not. I've got good judgment, and I know you've got nothing against me. Will you laugh me to sleep? I'm feeling very sleepy.

ANTONIO

Go to sleep, and listen to us laughing.

Everyone sleeps except ALONSO, SEBASTIAN, and ANTONIO.

ALONSO

What, everybody falls asleep so fast? I wish I could sleep too—it would stop me from thinking. Come to think of it, I am feeling sleepy.

SEBASTIAN

In that case you should sleep. People in grief need a good sleep. It doesn't come to them often, but when it does come they should enjoy it.

ANTONIO

The two of us will guard you while you sleep, my lord, and keep you safe.

ALONSO

Thank you. I'm terribly sleepy.

He falls asleep.

ARIEL exits.

SEBASTIAN
What a strange drowsiness possesses them!

ANTONIO
It is the quality o' th' climate.

SEBASTIAN
                                                    Why
Doth it not then our eyelids sink? I find not
190   Myself disposed to sleep.

ANTONIO
                                        Nor I. My spirits are nimble.
They fell together all, as by consent.
They dropped, as by a thunderstroke. What might,
Worthy Sebastian, O, what might—? No more.—
And yet methinks I see it in thy face,
195   What thou shouldst be. Th' occasion speaks thee, and
My strong imagination sees a crown
Dropping upon thy head.

SEBASTIAN
                                        What, art thou waking?

ANTONIO
Do you not hear me speak?

SEBASTIAN
                                        I do, and surely
It is a sleepy language, and thou speak'st
200   Out of thy sleep. What is it thou didst say?
This is a strange repose, to be asleep
With eyes wide open, standing, speaking, moving,
And yet so fast asleep.

ANTONIO
                                        Noble Sebastian,
Thou let'st thy fortune sleep—die, rather—wink'st
205   Whiles thou art waking.

SEBASTIAN
                                        Thou dost snore distinctly.
There's meaning in thy snores.

SEBASTIAN

How strange that they all got so sleepy!

ANTONIO

There must be something in the air here.

SEBASTIAN

So why aren't our eyelids heavy? I'm not sleepy at all.

ANTONIO

Me neither. I'm wide awake. They all fell asleep together, as if they'd planned it. Like they'd all been struck by lightning. What might happen, Sebastian, what might happen if—No, it's time for me to shut up.— But still, I think I can see in your face what you ought to be. Opportunity's knocking for you, and in my imagination I see a crown dropping onto your head.

SEBASTIAN

Are you dreaming or awake?

ANTONIO

Don't you hear me speaking?

SEBASTIAN

I do, and it sounds like you're talking in your sleep. What did you say? It's weird for you to be dreaming with your eyes wide open—standing, talking, moving, but sound asleep.

ANTONIO

Good Sebastian, you're the one who's sleeping if you let this opportunity pass you by without acting on it.

SEBASTIAN

You're snoring, but it sounds like you're talking. There's meaning in your snoring.

ANTONIO
> I am more serious than my custom. You
> Must be so too if heed me, which to do
> Trebles thee o'er.

SEBASTIAN
>   Well, I am standing water.

ANTONIO
210   I'll teach you how to flow.

SEBASTIAN
>   Do so. To ebb
> Hereditary sloth instructs me.

ANTONIO
>   Oh,
> If you but knew how you the purpose cherish
> Whiles thus you mock it! How, in stripping it,
> You more invest it! Ebbing men indeed
215   Most often do so near the bottom run
> By their own fear or sloth.

SEBASTIAN
>   Prithee, say on.
> The setting of thine eye and cheek proclaim
> A matter from thee, and a birth indeed
> Which throes thee much to yield.

ANTONIO
>   Thus, sir:
220   Although this lord of weak remembrance—this,
> Who shall be of as little memory
> When he is earthed—hath here almost persuade
> (For he's a spirit of persuasion only,
> Professes to persuade) the king his son's alive,
225   'Tis as impossible that he's undrowned
> And he that sleeps here swims.

ANTONIO

I'm not kidding when I say this, I'm not joking around like usual. You should be serious too when you listen to what I'm saying. You can become a great man if you listen to me.

SEBASTIAN

I'm hanging on every word you say.

ANTONIO

You need to do more than hang around—you have to act. I'll show you how.

SEBASTIAN

You need to. I'm lazy by nature.

ANTONIO

Oh, if you only knew how close to success you are, even while you make fun of what I'm telling you! The more you joke about it, the more clearly I feel how serious it is! Lazy people end up at the bottom, and you deserve to be at the top.

SEBASTIAN

Please, tell me more. There's something in your expression that tells me you have something serious to say, and you're having a lot of difficulty saying it.

ANTONIO

This is what I'm saying. *(points at* GONZALO*)* Although this lord who has such a bad memory—and who will be forgotten by the world when he's dead and buried—almost succeeded in convincing the king that his son's alive, it's impossible that he survived. It's as far from the truth as saying this sleeping man is swimming.

SEBASTIAN
                                              I have no hope
That he's undrowned.

ANTONIO
                                        Oh, out of that "no hope"
What great hope have you! No hope that way is
Another way so high a hope that even
230   Ambition cannot pierce a wink beyond,
But doubt discovery there. Will you grant with me
That Ferdinand is drowned?

SEBASTIAN
                                              He's gone.

ANTONIO
                                                Then, tell me,
Who's the next heir of Naples?

SEBASTIAN
                                              Claribel.

ANTONIO
She that is Queen of Tunis; she that dwells
235   Ten leagues beyond man's life; she that from Naples
Can have no note, unless the sun were post—
The man i' th' moon's too slow—till newborn chins
Be rough and razorable; she that from whom
We all were sea-swallowed, though some cast again,
240   And by that destiny to perform an act
Whereof what's past is prologue, what to come
In yours and my discharge.

SEBASTIAN
                                        What stuff is this? How say you?
'Tis true, my brother's daughter's Queen of Tunis,
So is she heir of Naples, 'twixt which regions
245   There is some space.

ANTONIO
                                        A space whose every cubit
Seems to cry out, "How shall that Claribel
Measure us back to Naples? Keep in Tunis,

SEBASTIAN

Yes, I'm sure he's dead. I've got no hope that he survived.

ANTONIO

But in that "no hope" there are great hopes for you! That "no hope" means you're on the way to glory so brilliant you couldn't even imagine it, no matter how ambitious you were. Do you agree that Ferdinand must have drowned?

SEBASTIAN

He's dead.

ANTONIO

So, in that case, tell me who's next in line to inherit the kingdom of Naples?

SEBASTIAN

Claribel, his daughter.

ANTONIO

The one who's now Queen of Tunis, living at the edge of the world, out of reach of mail service. It takes a letter longer to reach her than it takes a baby boy to grow old enough to shave. Claribel who was the cause of our shipwreck, which a few of us survived—she was destined to give us an opportunity that we are destined to act on.

SEBASTIAN

What in the world are you talking about? It's true that my brother's daughter is Queen of Tunis, and heir of Naples. And it's true those two places are far apart.

ANTONIO

So far that every foot of distance between them seems to shout, "It's too far for Claribel to come back to Naples. Let her stay in Tunis and give Sebastian a

And let Sebastian wake." Say this were death
That now hath seized them. Why, they were no worse
250   Than now they are. There be that can rule Naples
As well as he that sleeps, lords that can prate
As amply and unnecessarily
As this Gonzalo. I myself could make
A chough of as deep chat. Oh, that you bore
255   The mind that I do, what a sleep were this
For your advancement! Do you understand me?

SEBASTIAN
Methinks I do.

ANTONIO
               And how does your content
Tender your own good fortune?

SEBASTIAN
                   I remember
You did supplant your brother Prospero.

ANTONIO
                        True.
260   And look how well my garments sit upon me,
Much feater than before. My brother's servants
Were then my fellows. Now they are my men.

SEBASTIAN
But, for your conscience?

ANTONIO
Ay, sir. Where lies that? If 'twere a kibe,
265   'Twould put me to my slipper. But I feel not
This deity in my bosom. Twenty consciences,
That stand 'twixt me and Milan, candied be they
And melt ere they molest! Here lies your brother,
No better than the earth he lies upon,
270   If he were that which now he's like—that's dead—
Whom I, with this obedient steel, three inches of it,
Can lay to bed for ever; whiles you, doing thus,
To the perpetual wink for aye might put
This ancient morsel, this Sir Prudence, who

chance to start living." If these sleeping men were dead instead of sleeping, they'd be no worse off than they are now. There are a lot of men who can rule Naples just as well as this sleeping guy here can. There are a lot of men who babble nonsense as well as Gonzalo. I could do it myself. Oh, I wish you understood what I'm saying—you'd see how you're missing out on a great opportunity for yourself! Do you even get what I'm saying?

SEBASTIAN

I think I do.

ANTONIO

And does this prospect of good fortune make you happy?

SEBASTIAN

I remember you took the throne from your brother Prospero.

ANTONIO

Yes I did, and look how good I look in my new role— much better than before. My brother's servants used to be my equals. Now they work for me.

SEBASTIAN

But what about your guilty conscience?

ANTONIO

Yes. What guilty conscience? I don't feel anything. If my feet were cold, I'd put my slippers on, but I don't feel any pangs of guilt. If there were twenty guilty consciences between me and the dukedom, they'd melt away to nothing before they caused me any trouble. Here's your brother sleeping, worth no more than the dirt he's lying on. If he were as dead as he appears to be now—and I could quickly make him dead with this sword of mine—he wouldn't stand in our way. As

275 Should not upbraid our course. For all the rest,
They'll take suggestion as a cat laps milk.
They'll tell the clock to any business that
We say befits the hour.

SEBASTIAN
                                    Thy case, dear friend,
Shall be my precedent. As thou got'st Milan,
280 I'll come by Naples. Draw thy sword. One stroke
Shall free thee from the tribute which thou payest.
And I the king shall love thee.

ANTONIO
                                    Draw together.
And when I rear my hand, do you the like,
To fall it on Gonzalo.

ANTONIO and SEBASTIAN draw their swords

SEBASTIAN
                                    O, but one word.
(speaks quietly to ANTONIO)

Enter ARIEL invisible, with music and song

ARIEL
285 *(to GONZALO)* My master through his art foresees the danger
That you, his friend, are, and sends me forth—
For else his project dies—to keep them living.
(sings in GONZALO's ear)

        While you here do snoring lie,
        Open-eyed conspiracy
290   *His time doth take.*
        If of life you keep a care,
        Shake off slumber and beware.
        Awake, awake!

for the other men, we can make them believe anything we choose. They'll set their watches to whatever time we say.

SEBASTIAN

You'll be my role model. Just as you got Milan, I'll get Naples. Take out your sword. With one cut you can be through paying money to Naples. And as king I'll love you forever.

ANTONIO

You take out your sword too. When I raise my hand, you do the same, and bring it down on Gonzalo's head.

ANTONIO and SEBASTIAN take out their swords.

SEBASTIAN

Oh, but there's one more thing to tell you. *(he speaks quietly to ANTONIO)*

ARIEL enters, invisible, singing and playing music.

ARIEL

(to GONZALO) With his magic powers my master can see the dangers that you are in, my friend. So he sent me to make sure these men survive—and to guarantee his plans succeed. *(sings in GONZALO's ear)*

> *While you lie here snoring,*
> *Men are plotting against you.*
> *If you want to stay alive,*
> *Wake up and beware.*
> *Wake up, wake up!*

ANTONIO
Then let us both be sudden.

GONZALO
(waking and seeing them)
295   Now, good angels preserve the king!

ALONSO
(waking) Why, how now? Ho, awake!

All wake

Why are you drawn?
Wherefore this ghastly looking?

GONZALO
What's the matter?

SEBASTIAN
Whiles we stood here securing your repose,
300   Even now, we heard a hollow burst of bellowing
Like bulls, or rather lions. Did 't not wake you?
It struck mine ear most terribly.

ALONSO
I heard nothing.

ANTONIO
Oh, 'twas a din to fright a monster's ear,
To make an earthquake! Sure, it was the roar
305   Of a whole herd of lions.

ALONSO
Heard you this, Gonzalo?

GONZALO
Upon mine honor, sir, I heard a humming,
And that a strange one too, which did awake me.
I shaked you, sir, and cried. As mine eyes opened,
I saw their weapons drawn. There was a noise,
310   That's verily. 'Tis best we stand upon our guard,

ANTONIO

Let's act quickly.

GONZALO

(waking and seeing them) God help the king! Save him!

ALONSO

(waking up) Hey, what's this, what's going on? Wake up! Why are your swords out? Why do you look like that?

Everyone wakes up.

GONZALO

What's this all about?

SEBASTIAN

While we were here guarding you as you slept, we heard a loud roar that sounded like bulls, or lions. Didn't you hear it? We heard it very clearly.

ALONSO

I didn't hear anything.

ANTONIO

Oh, it was a monstrous roar, to make the earth tremble! I'm sure there was a herd of lions nearby.

ALONSO

Did you hear this, Gonzalo?

GONZALO

It's true I heard a humming sound, a strange one, which woke me up. I shook you and shouted at you, sir. When I opened my eyes, I saw their swords out. There was a noise, that's certainly true. We should either be on guard here constantly or move to a different camp. Let's draw our own swords too.

Or that we quit this place. Let's draw our weapons.

ALONSO
Lead off this ground, and let's make further search
For my poor son.

GONZALO
                    Heavens keep him from these beasts!
For he is, sure, i' th' island.

ALONSO
                    Lead away.

ARIEL
315   *(aside)* Prospero my lord shall know what I have done.
So, King, go safely on to seek thy son.

Exeunt

ALONSO

Lead us away from this area. We can search for my poor son while we're at it.

GONZALO

I hope those lions stay far away from him. I'm sure he's somewhere on the island.

ALONSO

Get us out of here.

ARIEL

(to himself) My lord Prospero will know what I've done. So go ahead, King, and look for your son.

They exit.

ACT 2, SCENE 2

Enter CALIBAN *with a burden of wood*
A noise of thunder heard

CALIBAN
All the infections that the sun sucks up
From bogs, fens, flats, on Prosper fall and make him
By inchmeal a disease! His spirits hear me
And yet I needs must curse. But they'll nor pinch,
5   Fright me with urchin-shows, pitch me i' th' mire,
Nor lead me like a firebrand in the dark
Out of my way, unless he bid 'em. But
For every trifle are they set upon me,
Sometime like apes that mow and chatter at me,
10 And after bite me, then like hedgehogs which
Lie tumbling in my barefoot way and mount
Their pricks at my footfall. Sometime am I
All wound with adders who with cloven tongues
Do hiss me into madness.

Enter TRINCULO

Lo, now, lo!
15 Here comes a spirit of his, and to torment me
For bringing wood in slowly. I'll fall flat.
Perchance he will not mind me.
(lies down, covered by his gaberdine)

TRINCULO
Here's neither bush nor shrub to bear off any weather at all.
And another storm brewing, I hear it sing i' th' wind. Yond
20 same black cloud, yond huge one, looks like a foul bombard
that would shed his liquor. If it should thunder as it did
before, I know not where to hide my head. Yond same cloud
cannot choose but fall by pailfuls. *(sees* CALIBAN*)*

ACT 2, SCENE 2

CALIBAN *enters with a load of wood. A noise of thunder is heard.*

CALIBAN

I hope all the diseases that breed in swamps and marshes infect Prospero, inch by inch, until he's nothing but a walking disease! His spirits are listening to me, but I can't help cursing him anyway. They won't pinch me, frighten me, push me in the mud, or mislead me unless he tells them to. But he sends them to punish me for every little thing. Sometimes his spirits take the form of apes, grimacing and chattering at me and then biting me; sometimes they come like porcupines, my feet as I walk. Sometimes snakes wrap around me, hissing at me with their forked tongues till I go crazy.

TRINCULO *enters.*

Hey, look over there! Here comes one of his spirits to torture me for taking so long to bring the wood back. I'll lie down and hide. Maybe he won't see me. *(he lies down and covers himself with his cloak)*

TRINCULO

There are no bushes or shrubs to protect me from the weather here. And there's another storm brewing—I can hear it in the way the wind whistles. That huge black cloud over there looks like a filthy liquor jug that's about to pour out its contents. It won't be able to help pouring rain down by the bucket-full. *(he sees CALIBAN)*

25   What have we here? A man or a fish? Dead or alive? A fish.
He smells like a fish, a very ancient and fish-like smell, a
kind of not-of-the-newest poor-john. A strange fish! Were
I in England now, as once I was, and had but this fish
painted, not a holiday fool there but would give a piece of
silver. There would this monster make a man. Any strange
30   beast there makes a man. When they will not give a doit to
relieve a lame beggar, they will lay out ten to see a dead
Indian. Legged like a man and his fins like arms! Warm, o'
my troth. I do now let loose my opinion, hold it no longer:
this is no fish, but an islander that hath lately suffered by a
35   thunderbolt.

    Thunder

    Alas, the storm is come again! My best way is to creep
under his gaberdine. There is no other shelter hereabouts.
Misery acquaints a man with strange bedfellows. I will here
shroud till the dregs of the storm be past.
    (crawls under gaberdine)

    Enter STEPHANO, *singing*

STEPHANO
    (sings)
        I shall no more to sea, to sea,
        Here shall I die ashore—
40   This is a very scurvy tune to sing at a man's funeral.
Well, here's my comfort. *(drinks, sings)*
        The master, the swabber, the boatswain, and I,
        The gunner and his mate
        Loved Mall, Meg, and Marian, and Margery,
        But none of us cared for Kate.
        For she had a tongue with a tang,

What do we have here, a man or a fish? Whew, he stinks like a fish—an old salted fish, not a fresh-caught one. A strange fish. If I were in England now, like I was once, and I had even a painted picture of this fish, every fool there would give me a piece of silver to look at it. In England this strange monster would be just like a man. Any strange beast there can be considered a man. The men there won't give a penny to a lame beggar, but they'll pay ten cents to look at a freak show exhibit. This guy has legs like a man but fins for arms! And he's still warm, by God. I guess this is not a fish, but a native who got struck by lightning just now.

Thunder.

Oh, here comes the storm again. The best thing to do is crawl under his cloak. There's no other shelter around here. In emergencies you meet the strangest folks. I'll just stay here till the storm passes. *(he crawls under* CALIBAN'*s cloak)*

STEPHANO *enters, singing.*

STEPHANO

(sings)

> *I'll never go to sea again,*
> *I'll die here on shore—*

This is a rotten song to sing at a man's funeral. At least I've got some booze to comfort me. *(he drinks and sings)*

> *The master, the deck-washer, the boatswain, and*
> *I,*
> *The gunman and his friend,*
> *We loved Moll, Meg, Marian, and Margery*
> *But none of us cared for Kate.*
> *Kate had a gutter mouth,*

Would cry to a sailor, "Go hang!"
She loved not the savor of tar nor of pitch,
Yet a tailor might scratch her where'er she did itch.
Then to sea, boys, and let her go hang!
This is a scurvy tune too. But here's my comfort.
(drinks)

CALIBAN

Do not torment me. Oh!

STEPHANO

What's the matter? Have we devils here? Do you put tricks upon 's with savages and men of Ind, ha? I have not 'scaped
45   drowning to be afeard now of your four legs. Or it hath been said, "As proper a man as ever went on four legs cannot make him give ground," and it shall be said so again while Stephano breathes at' nostrils.

CALIBAN

The spirit torments me. Oh!

STEPHANO

50   This is some monster of the isle with four legs who hath got, as I take it, an ague. Where the devil should he learn our language? I will give him some relief if it be but for that. If I can recover him and keep him tame and get to Naples with him, he's a present for any emperor that ever trod on neat's
55   leather.

CALIBAN

Do not torment me, prithee. I'll bring my wood home faster.

STEPHANO

He's in his fit now and does not talk after the wisest. He shall taste of my bottle. If he have never drunk wine afore,
60   it will go near to remove his fit. If I can recover him and keep him tame, I will not take too much for him. He shall pay for him that hath him, and that soundly.

> And would shout to sailors, "Go to hell!"
> She didn't like ship smells like tar,
> But liked it okay when a tailor took her to bed.
> So go to sea, boys, and let her go to hell!
> That's a rotten song too. But here's something to
>   comfort me.

(he drinks)

CALIBAN

Don't hurt me. Oh!

STEPHANO

What's going on? Do we have devils on the island?
Are you playing tricks on me by showing me savages
and uncivilized men from the Indies, ha? I didn't survive a shipwreck so I could be scared of your four legs
now. I'll never run away from any ordinary man who
walks on four legs like the rest of us.

Stephano speaks nonsense because he is drunk.

CALIBAN

The spirit is torturing me. Oh!

STEPHANO

This is some monster of the island, with four legs, who
seems to me to have some kind of ache. How the hell
does he know our language? I'll help out, if only
because he speaks the same language as me. If I can
cure him from his fever and tame him, and get him
back to Naples, he'd make a great present for any
emperor.

CALIBAN

Don't hurt me, please. I promise I'll carry the wood
faster.

STEPHANO

He's having a fit and talking nonsense. I'll give him
some liquor. If he's never drunk it before, it'll help
soothe his fever. If I can tame him, I'll charge as much
as I can get for him. He'll bring a lot of money to the
person who owns him, that's for sure.

CALIBAN
> Thou dost me yet but little hurt. Thou wilt anon, I know it
> by thy trembling. Now Prosper works upon thee.

STEPHANO
> *(trying to give* CALIBAN *drink)*
65 Come on your ways. Open your mouth. Here is that which
> will give language to you, cat. Open your mouth. This will
> shake your shaking, I can tell you, and that soundly. You
> cannot tell who's your friend. Open your chaps again.

TRINCULO
> I should know that voice. It should be—But he is drowned,
70 and these are devils. Oh, defend me!

STEPHANO
> Four legs and two voices—a most delicate monster. His
> forward voice now is to speak well of his friend. His
> backward voice is to utter foul speeches and to detract. If all
> the wine in my bottle will recover him, I will help his ague.
75 Come.

> CALIBAN *drinks*

> Amen! I will pour some in thy other mouth.

TRINCULO
> Stephano!

STEPHANO
> Doth thy other mouth call me? Mercy, mercy! This is a
> devil, and no monster. I will leave him. I have no long
80 spoon.

TRINCULO
> Stephano! If thou beest Stephano, touch me and speak to
> me. For I am Trinculo—be not afeard—thy good friend
> Trinculo.

STEPHANO
> If thou beest Trinculo, come forth. I'll pull thee by the
85 lesser legs. If any be Trinculo's legs, these are they.
> *(pulls* TRINCULO *out from under the gaberdine)*

CALIBAN

> You haven't hurt me much yet, but you will soon, I can tell by your trembling. Prospero sent you here.

STEPHANO

> *(trying to make* CALIBAN *drink)* Come on, open your mouth. This'll help you talk. Open up. This'll stop you from trembling—I can tell you that for sure. *(CALIBAN drinks)* You don't even know who your friends are. Open up that mouth again.

TRINCULO

> I almost recognize that voice. It's—But he's drowned, and these guys are devils. Oh, God help me!

STEPHANO

> Four legs and two voices—a very special monster. One voice speaks well and talks about his friend. The other voice is harsh and abusive. I can charge even more for this. If it takes all the wine in my bottle, I'll cure him. Come on. *(CALIBAN drinks)* That's good! Now I'll pour some in your other mouth.

TRINCULO

> Stephano!

STEPHANO

> Is your other mouth calling my name? Mercy, mercy! This isn't a monster, it's a devil. I'll leave him alone. I have no interest in getting mixed up with the devil.

TRINCULO

> Stephano! If you're Stephano, touch me and speak to me. I'm Trinculo—don't be scared—your good friend Trinculo.

STEPHANO

> If you're Trinculo, then come out. I'll pull on these smaller legs. If any legs here are Trinculo's, these are. *(he pulls* TRINCULO *out from under the cloak)* Well, what

Thou art very Trinculo indeed! How camest thou to be the
siege of this mooncalf? Can he vent Trinculos?

TRINCULO

I took him to be killed with a thunderstroke. But art thou
not drowned, Stephano? I hope now thou art not drowned.
90   Is the storm overblown? I hid me under the dead
mooncalf's gaberdine for fear of the storm. And art thou
living, Stephano? O Stephano, two Neapolitans 'scaped!
(dances STEPHANO *about)*

STEPHANO

Prithee, do not turn me about. My stomach is not constant.

CALIBAN

(aside) These be fine things, an if they be not sprites. That's
95   a brave god and bears celestial liquor. I will kneel to him.

STEPHANO

(to TRINCULO*)* How didst thou 'scape? How camest thou
hither? Swear by this bottle how thou camest hither. I
escaped upon a butt of sack which the sailors heaved
o'erboard, by this bottle, which I made of the bark of a tree
100   with mine own hands since I was cast ashore.

CALIBAN

(to STEPHANO*)* I'll swear upon that bottle to be thy true
subject, for the liquor is not earthly.

STEPHANO

(to TRINCULO*)* Here. Swear then how thou escapedst.

TRINCULO

Swum ashore, man, like a duck. I can swim like a duck, I'll
105   be sworn.

STEPHANO

Here, kiss the book. Though thou canst swim like a duck,
thou art made like a goose.

do you know, you *are* Trinculo! How did you end up as this monster's dung? Does he crap Trinculos?

TRINCULO

I thought he was dead, struck by lightning. But aren't you drowned, Stephano? I hope you're not drowned. Has the storm passed? I hid under this monster's cloak to get out of the storm. Are you really alive, Stephano? Oh, Stephano, two men from Naples survived! (TRIN-CULO *dances* STEPHANO *around.*)

STEPHANO

Please stop turning me around. My stomach's a little upset.

CALIBAN

(to himself) These are beautiful creatures, if they're not spirits. He's a good god, who brings liquor from the heavens. I will worship him.

STEPHANO

(to TRINCULO*)* How did you survive? How did you get here? Tell me the truth, swear on this bottle of wine. I made it out of tree bark after I washed ashore. I myself floated here on a barrel of wine that the sailors tossed overboard.

CALIBAN

(to STEPHANO*)* I'll swear by that wine bottle to be your true subject. You must be a god, since your liquor is out of this world.

STEPHANO

(to TRINCULO*)* Here. Swear, and tell me how you survived.

TRINCULO

I swam ashore like a duck. I can swim like a duck, I swear.

STEPHANO

Here, kiss the Bible and swear. You may swim like a duck, but you look more like a goose.

Stephano jokingly describes taking a drink from the bottle as "kissing the Bible."

TRINCULO *drinks*

TRINCULO
> O Stephano, hast any more of this?

STEPHANO
> The whole butt, man. My cellar is in a rock by th' seaside
110 where my wine is hid.—How now, mooncalf? How does
> thine ague?

CALIBAN
> Hast thou not dropped from heaven?

STEPHANO
> Out o' th' moon, I do assure thee. I was the man i'
> the moon when time was.

CALIBAN
115 I have seen thee in her and I do adore thee. My mistress
> showed me thee and thy dog and thy bush.

STEPHANO
> Come, swear to that, kiss the book. I will furnish it anon
> with new contents, swear.

CALIBAN *drinks*

TRINCULO
> By this good light, this is a very shallow monster. I afeard
120 of him! A very weak monster. The man i' th' moon! A most
> poor credulous monster.—Well drawn, monster, in good
> sooth!

CALIBAN
> *(to* STEPHANO*)* I'll show thee every fertile inch o' th' island.
> And I will kiss thy foot. I prithee, be my god.

TRINCULO
125 By this light, a most perfidious and drunken monster.
> When 's god's asleep, he'll rob his bottle.

TRINCULO *drinks.*

TRINCULO

Oh Stephano, do you have any more of that wine?

STEPHANO

I've got the whole barrel, man. I live in a cave by the seaside, where I keep the barrel hidden.—Hey, monster, how's your fever?

CALIBAN

You come from heaven, don't you?

STEPHANO

No, from the moon, I'm telling you. I used to be the man in the moon a long time ago.

CALIBAN

Oh, I've seen you in the moon, and I worship you. My mistress showed me you in the moon and your dog and your bush.

STEPHANO

Come on, swear to it. Kiss the Bible and swear it. I'm going to fill the bottle up again soon.

CALIBAN *drinks.*

TRINCULO

When you get a good look at him, you see he's not much of a monster. I can't believe I was scared of him! A pretty pathetic monster. The man in the moon! What a poor, gullible monster.—That was a nice big gulp, monster!

CALIBAN

(to STEPHANO*)* I'll show you every inch of the island, and I'll kiss your feet. I beg you, please be my god.

TRINCULO

What a lying, drunken monster. When his god falls asleep, the monster will snatch his wine bottle.

CALIBAN
> *(to* STEPHANO*)* I'll kiss thy foot. I'll swear myself thy
> subject.

STEPHANO
> Come on then. Down, and swear.

TRINCULO
130 > I shall laugh myself to death at this puppy-headed monster.
> A most scurvy monster. I could find in my heart to beat
> him—

STEPHANO
> *(to* CALIBAN*)* Come, kiss.

TRINCULO
> But that the poor monster's in drink. An abominable
135 > monster!

CALIBAN
> I'll show thee the best springs. I'll pluck thee berries.
> I'll fish for thee and get thee wood enough.
> A plague upon the tyrant that I serve!
> I'll bear him no more sticks, but follow thee,
140 > Thou wondrous man.

TRINCULO
> A most ridiculous monster, to make a wonder of a poor
> drunkard.

CALIBAN
> *(to* STEPHANO*)* I prithee, let me bring thee where crabs grow.
> And I with my long nails will dig thee pignuts,
145 > Show thee a jay's nest, and instruct thee how
> To snare the nimble marmoset. I'll bring thee
> To clustering filberts, and sometimes I'll get thee
> Young scamels from the rock. Wilt thou go with me?

STEPHANO
> I prithee now, lead the way without any more talking.—
150 > Trinculo, the king and all our company else being drowned,
> we will inherit here.—Here, bear my bottle.—Fellow
> Trinculo, we'll fill him by and by again.

CALIBAN

(to STEPHANO*)* I'll kiss your feet. I'll vow to be your faithful subject.

STEPHANO

Come on, then. Get down and swear it.

TRINCULO

I'm going to laugh myself to death over this silly monster. A rotten, foolish monster. I could find it in my heart to beat him—

STEPHANO

Come on, kiss my feet.

TRINCULO

Except the poor monster's drunk. An awful monster!

CALIBAN

I'll show you where to get fresh water. I'll pick berries for you. I'll fish for you and get you plenty of firewood. The tyrant I'm serving now can go to hell! I won't get any more wood for him. I'm serving you now, you wonderful man.

TRINCULO

What a silly monster, to think a poor drunk is wonderful.

CALIBAN

(to STEPHANO*)* I beg you, let me show where you can find crabs to eat. I'll use my long fingernails to dig edible roots for you, find you a bird's nest, and teach you how to catch a nimble monkey. I'll take you to clusters of hazelnuts, and sometimes I'll catch birds for you on the rocks. Will you come with me?

STEPHANO

Show us the way without further delay.—Trinculo, since the king and all our comrades are drowned, we're the heirs of this place.—Here, carry my wine bottle.—Trinculo, my buddy, we'll get that bottle refilled soon enough.

CALIBAN
(sings drunkenly)
Farewell, master! Farewell, farewell.

TRINCULO
A howling monster, a drunken monster.

CALIBAN
(sings)
155 *No more dams I'll make for fish,*
Nor fetch in firing
At requiring,
Nor scrape trencher, nor wash dish.
'Ban, 'Ban, Ca-caliban
160 *Has a new master. Get a new man.*
Freedom, high-day, high-day, freedom, freedom, high-
day, freedom!

STEPHANO
O brave monster! Lead the way.

Exeunt

CALIBAN

> (*sings drunkenly*)
>> *Goodbye, master! Goodbye, goodbye.*

TRINCULO

A loud-mouthed, drunken monster.

CALIBAN

> (*sings*)
>> *I won't build you any more dams to catch fish,*
>> *Or fetch you firewood when you order me to,*
>> *Or clean the plates, or wash dishes.*
>> *'Ban, 'ban, Ca-caliban*
>> *Has a new master. So get a new servant.*
>> *Freedom, what a wonderful day, wonderful day,*
>>> *freedom, freedom, wonderful day, free-*
>>> *dom!*

STEPHANO

Good monster! Show us the way.

> *They exit.*

ACT THREE

SCENE 1

Enter FERDINAND *bearing a log*

FERDINAND
There be some sports are painful, and their labor
Delight in them sets off. Some kinds of baseness
Are nobly undergone. And most poor matters
Point to rich ends. This my mean task
5   Would be as heavy to me as odious, but
The mistress which I serve quickens what's dead
And makes my labors pleasures. Oh, she is
Ten times more gentle than her father's crabbed,
And he's composed of harshness. I must remove
10   Some thousands of these logs and pile them up,
Upon a sore injunction. My sweet mistress
Weeps when she sees me work, and says such baseness
Had never like executor. I forget,
But these sweet thoughts do even refresh my labors,
15   Most busiest when I do it.

Enter MIRANDA, *and* PROSPERO *unseen*

MIRANDA
                    Alas now, pray you,
Work not so hard. I would the lightning had
Burnt up those logs that you are enjoined to pile!
Pray, set it down and rest you. When this burns,
'Twill weep for having wearied you. My father
20   Is hard at study. Pray now, rest yourself.
He's safe for these three hours.

ACT THREE
SCENE 1

FERDINAND *enters, carrying a log.*

FERDINAND

Some games are painful, but their discomfort makes them more fun. Some kinds of lowly activities are done for noble reasons. And you can do poor things that lead to rich results. This hard work would be boring and nasty to me, but I'm working for a mistress who makes me enjoy my labor. Oh, she's ten times nicer than her father is mean, and he's the height of crabbiness. I have thousands of logs to take away and pile up, on strict orders from him. My sweet darling cries when she sees me work and tells me that such a wonderful man never performed such lowly tasks before. These sweet thoughts relieve me and refresh me, especially when I'm slaving away busily.

MIRANDA *enters, followed by* PROSPERO *at a distance, unobserved.*

MIRANDA

Now, please, I beg you, don't work so hard. I wish the lightning had burned up all those logs that you've been ordered to stack! Please put that log down and rest a while. When this wood burns, it'll weep for making you tired. My father's studying hard, so he won't see you. So please rest. We're safe from my father for at least three hours.

FERDINAND
                                        O most dear mistress,
The sun will set before I shall discharge
What I must strive to do.

MIRANDA
                                        If you'll sit down,
I'll bear your logs the while. Pray, give me that.
25   I'll carry it to the pile.

FERDINAND
                                        No, precious creature.
I had rather crack my sinews, break my back,
Than you should such dishonor undergo
While I sit lazy by.

MIRANDA
                                        It would become me
As well as it does you, and I should do it
30   With much more ease, for my good will is to it
And yours it is against.

PROSPERO
   (aside)   Poor worm, thou art infected!
This visitation shows it.

MIRANDA
                                        You look wearily.

FERDINAND
No, noble mistress. 'Tis fresh morning with me
When you are by at night. I do beseech you—
35   Chiefly that I might set it in my prayers—
What is your name?

MIRANDA
                                        Miranda.—O my father,
I have broke your hest to say so!

FERDINAND
                                        Admired Miranda!
Indeed the top of admiration, worth
What's dearest to th' world! Full many a lady
40   I have eyed with best regard and many a time

FERDINAND

Oh, my dear mistress, I won't be able to finish this work until sunset at the earliest.

MIRANDA

If you sit down, I'll carry your logs a while. Please give me that. I'll take it over to the pile.

FERDINAND

No, my darling, I'd rather strain all my muscles and break my back than let you do work like this while I lounge around nearby.

MIRANDA

I'd be as right for the job as you are, and I'd do it more easily, since I'd have good will on my side.

PROSPERO

(to himself) You poor weak thing, you're in love! I can see it clearly now.

MIRANDA

You look tired.

FERDINAND

No, noble mistress, I'm as fresh as morning when you're near me, even at night. I beg you to tell me your name so I can use it in my prayers.

MIRANDA

Miranda.—Oh father, I've disobeyed you by telling him that!

FERDINAND

Miranda—the very name means "admired!" You are indeed admired, more than anything else in the world! I've looked at many ladies with pleasure, and been

Th' harmony of their tongues hath into bondage
Brought my too diligent ear. For several virtues
Have I liked several women. Never any
With so full soul but some defect in her
45   Did quarrel with the noblest grace she owed
And put it to the foil. But you, O you,
So perfect and so peerless, are created
Of every creature's best.

MIRANDA

                            I do not know
One of my sex, no woman's face remember—
50   Save, from my glass, mine own. Nor have I seen
More that I may call men than you, good friend,
And my dear father. How features are abroad
I am skill-less of, but, by my modesty,
The jewel in my dower, I would not wish
55   Any companion in the world but you,
Nor can imagination form a shape
Besides yourself to like of. But I prattle
Something too wildly, and my father's precepts
I therein do forget.

FERDINAND

                            I am in my condition
60   A prince, Miranda—I do think, a king;
I would, not so!—and would no more endure
This wooden slavery than to suffer
The flesh-fly blow my mouth. Hear my soul speak.
The very instant that I saw you did
65   My heart fly to your service, there resides
To make me slave to it, and for your sake
Am I this patient log-man.

MIRANDA

                            Do you love me?

FERDINAND
O heaven, O earth, bear witness to this sound
And crown what I profess with kind event

seduced by the sweet nothings they said to me. I've liked several women for their good qualities, but there was something wrong with each one that blotted her excellent qualities and cancelled them out. But with you it's different. You're perfect, without a rival in the world, made up of the best qualities of every creature.

MIRANDA

I've never known any woman or seen a woman's face—except my own in the mirror. And I've never met any men besides you and my father. I have no idea what people look like in other places, but I swear by my modesty, which I value above everything else, that I'd never want any companion in the world but you. I can't even imagine one. But listen to me chattering like crazy, and father always told me not to.

FERDINAND

I'm a prince by birth, Miranda—maybe even a king now; though I wish I weren't—and normally I wouldn't put up with carrying these logs any more than I'd let flies breed in my mouth. But I'll tell you something from my soul. The second I saw you, my heart rushed to serve you and be your slave, so here I am now, a patient log-man.

MIRANDA

Do you love me?

FERDINAND

Oh heaven, oh earth, witness what I'm about to say, and reward me if I tell the truth! If I'm lying, then

70   If I speak true! If hollowly, invert
      What best is boded me to mischief! I
      Beyond all limit of what else i' th' world
      Do love, prize, honor you.

MIRANDA
                                    I am a fool
      To weep at what I am glad of.

PROSPERO
      (aside)   Fair encounter
75   Of two most rare affections! Heavens rain grace
      On that which breeds between 'em!

FERDINAND
      Wherefore weep you?

MIRANDA
      At mine unworthiness, that dare not offer
      What I desire to give, and much less take
80   What I shall die to want. But this is trifling,
      And all the more it seeks to hide itself
      The bigger bulk it shows. Hence, bashful cunning,
      And prompt me, plain and holy innocence!
      I am your wife if you will marry me.
85   If not, I'll die your maid. To be your fellow
      You may deny me, but I'll be your servant
      Whether you will or no.

FERDINAND
      My mistress, dearest, and I thus humble ever.

MIRANDA
      My husband, then?

FERDINAND
90   Ay, with a heart as willing
      As bondage e'er of freedom. Here's my hand.

MIRANDA
      And mine, with my heart in 't. And now farewell
      Till half an hour hence.

destroy all my prospects in life! More than anything else in the world, I love you, value you, and honor you.

MIRANDA

Look at me crying—what a fool I am to cry at what makes me happy.

PROSPERO

(to himself) What a pleasant meeting between two people truly in love! May heaven bless the feelings growing between them!

FERDINAND

Why are you crying?

MIRANDA

I'm crying at how unworthy I am to give you what I want to give you and to take what I'm dying to have. But it's a waste of time to say so. The more I try to hide what I'm feeling, the bigger it gets. Oh, stop being so bashful and tricky, Miranda, just be straightforward and innocent! I'll be your wife if you'll have me. Otherwise, I'll die a virgin, devoted to you. You can refuse to make me your spouse, but I'll be your servant whether you want me to or not.

FERDINAND

You'll be my wife, dearest, and I'll serve you forever.

MIRANDA

Will you be my husband, then?

FERDINAND

Yes, with a heart more eager to bear a husband's responsibilities than a slave ever wanted freedom. Take my hand, darling.

MIRANDA

Here's my hand, and my heart. And now goodbye. I'll see you again in half an hour.

FERDINAND
A thousand thousand!

Exeunt **FERDINAND** *and* **MIRANDA** *severally*

PROSPERO
95   So glad of this as they I cannot be,
Who are surprised withal. But my rejoicing
At nothing can be more. I'll to my book,
For yet ere supper-time must I perform
Much business appertaining.

Exit

FERDINAND

A million goodbyes to you.

MIRANDA and FERDINAND exit in opposite directions.

PROSPERO

I can't be as happy as they are at this moment, but nothing could make me any happier. Now it's time to get back to my studying, since I have a lot of serious business to take care of before dinner.

He exits.

ACT 3, SCENE 2

Enter CALIBAN, STEPHANO, *and* TRINCULO

STEPHANO

Tell not me. When the butt is out, we will drink water. Not a drop before. Therefore bear up and board 'em.—Servant-monster, drink to me.

TRINCULO

"Servant-monster"? The folly of this island. They say there's but five upon this isle. We are three of them. If th' other two be brained like us, the state totters.

STEPHANO

Drink, servant-monster, when I bid thee. Thy eyes are almost set in thy head.

TRINCULO

Where should they be set else? He were a brave monster indeed, if they were set in his tail.

STEPHANO

My man-monster hath drowned his tongue in sack. For my part, the sea cannot drown me. I swam, ere I could recover the shore, five and thirty leagues off and on. By this light, thou shalt be my lieutenant, monster, or my standard.

TRINCULO

Your lieutenant, if you list. He's no standard.

STEPHANO

We'll not run, Monsieur Monster.

TRINCULO

Nor go neither. But you'll lie like dogs, and yet say nothing neither.

ACT 3, SCENE 2

CALIBAN, STEPHANO, *and* TRINCULO *enter.*

STEPHANO

Don't tell me that. When the barrel's empty, we'll drink water. Not one drop sooner. Therefore, drink up.—Servant-monster, drink a toast to me.

TRINCULO

"Servant monster"? What a crazy island this is. They say there are only five people on it. We're three of them. If the other two are as loopy as we are, our country's in bad shape.

STEPHANO

Drink when I order you, servant-monster. Your eyes look like they've sunk into your head.

TRINCULO

Where else should his eyes be, if not in his head? He'd be quite a monster if his eyes were in his tail.

STEPHANO

My man—monster is so drunk he can't talk. As for me, no liquid can harm me, neither booze nor the whole sea itself. Before I could get to shore, I swam thirty-five leagues in it and still survived.—Monster, you'll be my lieutenant, or my flag-bearer.

1 league = 3 miles

TRINCULO

Lieutenant is better. He's not standing straight enough to hold a flag.

STEPHANO

We're not going to run in our army, Monsieur Monster.

TRINCULO

Or walk either. You'll just lie there like sleeping dogs and say nothing.

STEPHANO

20
> Mooncalf, speak once in thy life, if thou beest a good mooncalf.

CALIBAN

> How does thy honor? Let me lick thy shoe.
> *(indicates* TRINCULO*)* I'll not serve him. He's not valiant.

TRINCULO

> *(to* CALIBAN*)*
>
25
> Thou liest, most ignorant monster. I am in case to justle a constable. Why, thou deboshed fish, thou, was there ever man a coward that hath drunk so much sack as I today? Wilt thou tell a monstrous lie, being but half a fish and half a monster?

CALIBAN

> *(to* STEPHANO*)*
> Lo, how he mocks me! Wilt thou let him, mylord?

TRINCULO

> "Lord," quoth he? That a monster should be such a natural!

CALIBAN

> *(to* STEPHANO*)*
>
30
> Lo, lo, again! Bite him to death, I prithee.

STEPHANO

> Trinculo, keep a good tongue in your head. If you prove a mutineer, the next tree. The poor monster's my subject and he shall not suffer indignity.

CALIBAN

> I thank my noble lord. Wilt thou be pleased to hearken once
>
35
> again to the suit I made to thee?

STEPHANO

> Marry, will I. Kneel and repeat it. I will stand, and so shall Trinculo.

Enter ARIEL, *invisible*

STEPHANO

Monster sweetie, be a good monster and just speak once.

CALIBAN

How is your Highness? Let me lick your shoe. *(he points to* TRINCULO*)* I'll never serve that guy there. He's not courageous like you.

TRINCULO

(to CALIBAN*)* You're a liar, you ignorant monster. I'm courageous. I could shake up a police officer right now. You drunken fish, you, how could you call me a coward after all the booze I've drunk today? Do you tell such monstrous lies because you're half fish and half monster?

CALIBAN

(to STEPHANO*)* Look how he's making fun of me! Will you let him talk to me like, my lord?

TRINCULO

"Lord," he calls you? What an idiot that monster is!

CALIBAN

(to STEPHANO*)* There he goes again! Please, bite him to death, I'm begging you.

STEPHANO

Trinculo, speak politely. If you mutiny against me, I'll hang you from the next tree. This poor monster is my subject, and I will not allow him to be insulted.

CALIBAN

Thank you, my noble lord. Now would you please listen once again to the request I made to you earlier?

STEPHANO

Indeed, I will. Kneel and tell me again. I'll stand, and so will Trinculo.

ARIEL *enters, invisible.*

CALIBAN

(kneeling) As I told thee before, I am subject to a tyrant, a
sorcerer that by his cunning hath cheated me of the island.

ARIEL

40   Thou liest.

CALIBAN

(to TRINCULO*)*
Thou liest, thou jesting monkey, thou! I would my valiant
master would destroy thee. I do not lie.

STEPHANO

Trinculo, if you trouble him any more in 's tale, by this
hand, I will supplant some of your teeth.

TRINCULO

45   Why, I said nothing.

STEPHANO

Mum, then, and no more. Proceed.

CALIBAN

I say, by sorcery he got this isle.
From me he got it. If thy greatness will
Revenge it on him—for I know thou darest,
50   But this thing dare not—

STEPHANO

That's most certain.

CALIBAN

Thou shalt be lord of it and I'll serve thee.

STEPHANO

How now shall this be compassed?
Canst thou bring me to th' party?

CALIBAN

55   Yea, yea, my lord. I'll yield him thee asleep,
Where thou mayst knock a nail into his head.

ARIEL

Thou liest. Thou canst not.

CALIBAN

(kneeling) As I told you before, I'm enslaved to a tyrant, a magician who tricked me with magic spells and took my island from me.

ARIEL

You lie.

CALIBAN

(to TRINCULO*)* You're the liar, you big fat monkey. I wish my courageous master would kill you. I'm not lying.

STEPHANO

Trinculo, if you interrupt him any more, I swear I'll knock some teeth out of your head.

TRINCULO

I didn't say anything.

STEPHANO

Okay, just stay quiet. Go on.

CALIBAN

I was telling you he used witchcraft to take this island. He stole it from me. If your highness is willing, take revenge on him for that—because I know you're brave enough, I don't dare to—

STEPHANO

That's for sure.

CALIBAN

You'll be lord of the island then, and I'll be your servant.

STEPHANO

And how would we go about doing that? Can you bring me to him?

CALIBAN

Yes, yes, my lord. I'll take you to where he sleeps, and you can pound a nail into his head.

ARIEL

You lie. You can't do that.

CALIBAN
What a pied ninny's this!—Thou scurvy patch!—
I do beseech thy greatness, give him blows
60 And take his bottle from him. When that's gone,
He shall drink naught but brine, for I'll not show him
Where the quick freshes are.

STEPHANO
Trinculo, run into no further danger. Interrupt the monster
one word further, and, by this hand, I'll turn my mercy out
65 o' doors and make a stockfish of thee.

TRINCULO
Why, what did I? I did nothing. I'll go farther off.

STEPHANO
Didst thou not say he lied?

ARIEL
Thou liest.

STEPHANO
(to TRINCULO*)* Do I so? Take thou that.
(beats TRINCULO*)*
70 As you like this, give me the lie another time.

TRINCULO
I did not give the lie. Out o' your wits and hearing too? A
pox o' your bottle! This can sack and drinking do. A
murrain on your monster, and the devil take your fingers!

CALIBAN
Ha, ha, ha!

STEPHANO
75 Now, forward with your tale.—Prithee, stand farther off.

CALIBAN
Beat him enough. After a little time,
I'll beat him too.

STEPHANO
Stand farther.—Come, proceed.

CALIBAN

What an idiot this guy is!—You're a rotten piece of work!—I beg your highness, beat him up and take his wine bottle from him. When he loses that, he'll be drinking salt water, since I'll never tell him where the freshwater springs are.

STEPHANO

Trinculo, watch out. If you interrupt this monster with one more word, I'll beat you like a piece of salted fish.

TRINCULO

What did I do? I didn't do anything. I need to get away from you.

STEPHANO

Didn't you call him a liar?

ARIEL

You lie.

STEPHANO

(to TRINCULO*)* Oh, I did? Take that, then. *(he beats* TRINCULO*)* If you want more beatings like that, just accuse me of lying again.

TRINCULO

I didn't accuse you of lying. Are you out of your mind and deaf too? Damn your wine! This is what happens when you drink too much. Your monster can go to hell, and you can too!

CALIBAN

Ha, ha, ha!

STEPHANO

Now go ahead and tell me the rest of your story.— Please go stand farther away.

CALIBAN

Beat him up. After a little while, I'll beat him too.

STEPHANO

Stand farther away.— Come on, continue your story.

CALIBAN
  Why, as I told thee, 'tis a custom with him,
80 I' th' afternoon to sleep. There thou mayst brain him,
  Having first seized his books; or with a log
  Batter his skull; or paunch him with a stake;
  Or cut his weasand with thy knife. Remember
  First to possess his books, for without them
85 He's but a sot, as I am, nor hath not
  One spirit to command. They all do hate him
  As rootedly as I. Burn but his books.
  He has brave utensils—for so he calls them—
  Which when he has a house, he'll deck withal.
90 And that most deeply to consider is
  The beauty of his daughter. He himself
  Calls her a nonpareil. I never saw a woman,
  But only Sycorax my dam and she.
  But she as far surpasseth Sycorax
95 As great'st does least.

STEPHANO
          Is it so brave a lass?

CALIBAN
  Ay, lord. She will become thy bed, I warrant.
  And bring thee forth brave brood.

STEPHANO
  Monster, I will kill this man. His daughter and I will be
  king and queen—save our graces!—and Trinculo and
100 thyself shall be viceroys.—Dost thou like the plot,
  Trinculo?

TRINCULO
  Excellent.

STEPHANO
  Give me thy hand. I am sorry I beat thee. But while thou
  livest, keep a good tongue in thy head.

CALIBAN
105 Within this half hour will he be asleep. Wilt thou destroy
  him then?

CALIBAN

Just as I told you, he usually sleeps in the afternoon. At that time you can smash in his skull after seizing his books; or you can bash his skull with a log; or you can stab him in the belly; or cut his windpipe. Just remember to grab his books first, since without them he's just a poor fool like me, and can't command a single spirit. All the spirits hate him as much as I do. Be sure to burn his magic books. He has some wonderful home furnishings—that's what he calls them—that he'll use to decorate his house when he gets one. The most important thing for you to think about is how beautiful his daughter is. He says she has no equal. I never saw a woman except her and Sycorax, my mother. But Miranda is so much more beautiful, you can't even compare the two.

STEPHANO

Is she really that wonderful?

CALIBAN

Yes, my lord. She'll look good in your bed, and she'll produce some fine children too.

STEPHANO

Monster, I'll kill this man. His daughter and I will be king and queen—God protect us!—and you and Trinculo will be our governors.—Do you like that idea, Trinculo?

TRINCULO

Excellent.

STEPHANO

Give me your hand. I'm sorry I hit you. But try to control your speech.

CALIBAN

In a half an hour he'll be asleep. Will you kill him then?

STEPHANO
Ay, on mine honor.

ARIEL
(aside) This will I tell my master.

CALIBAN
Thou makest me merry. I am full of pleasure.
110 Let us be jocund. Will you troll the catch
You taught me but whilere?

STEPHANO
At thy request, monster, I will do reason, any reason.—
Come on, Trinculo, let us sing.
(sings)
Flout 'em and scout 'em,
115 And scout 'em and flout 'em.
Thought is free.

CALIBAN
That's not the tune.

ARIEL *plays the tune on a tabor and pipe*

STEPHANO
What is this same?

TRINCULO
This is the tune of our catch, played by the picture of
120 Nobody.

STEPHANO
If thou beest a man, show thyself in thy likeness. If thou
beest a devil, take 't as thou list.

TRINCULO
O, forgive me my sins!

STEPHANO
He that dies pays all debts.—I defy thee!—Mercy upon us!

CALIBAN
125 Art thou afeard?

STEPHANO

Yes, I swear.

ARIEL

(to himself) I'll tell my master this.

CALIBAN

You make me so happy. I'm full of joy. Let's be light-hearted. Will you sing the tune you taught me just a little while ago?

STEPHANO

I'll do anything you ask, monster, anything reasonable.—Come on, Trinculo, let's sing. *(he sings)*
> Dismiss 'em and ziss 'em
> And diss 'em and dismiss 'em.
> Thought is free.

CALIBAN

That's not the tune I had in mind.

ARIEL *plays the tune on a drum and a pipe.*

STEPHANO

What's this song?

TRINCULO

That's the melody, played by Nobody.

STEPHANO

(to the invisible musician) If you're a man, then let us see what you look like. If you're a devil, then go to hell.

TRINCULO

Oh, forgive all my sins!

STEPHANO

Dead men have to pay their debts.—I challenge you!—God help us.

CALIBAN

Are you scared?

STEPHANO

No, monster, not I.

CALIBAN

Be not afeard. The isle is full of noises,
Sounds, and sweet airs that give delight and hurt not.
Sometimes a thousand twangling instruments
130 Will hum about mine ears, and sometime voices
That, if I then had waked after long sleep,
Will make me sleep again. And then, in dreaming,
The clouds methought would open and show riches
Ready to drop upon me, that when I waked
135 I cried to dream again.

STEPHANO

This will prove a brave kingdom to me, where I shall have
my music for nothing.

CALIBAN

When Prospero is destroyed.

STEPHANO

That shall be by and by. I remember the story.

TRINCULO

140 The sound is going away. Let's follow it, and after do our
work.

STEPHANO

Lead, monster; we'll follow. I would I could see this
taborer. He lays it on.

TRINCULO

Wilt come? I'll follow, Stephano.

Exeunt

STEPHANO

No, monster, not me.

CALIBAN

Don't be scared. This island is full of noises, strange sounds and sweet melodies that make you feel good and don't hurt anyone. Sometimes I hear a thousand twanging instruments hum at my ears, and sometimes voices that send me back to sleep even if I had just woken up—and then I dreamed of clouds opening up and dropping such riches on me that when I woke up, I cried because I wanted to dream again.

STEPHANO

This'll be a wonderful kingdom to live in, where they play music for free.

CALIBAN

As soon as you kill Prospero.

STEPHANO

That'll happen soon enough. I remember the plan.

TRINCULO

The sound is going away. But let's follow it, and then do our dirty work afterward.

STEPHANO

Lead us, monster; we'll follow. I wish I could see this invisible drummer. He really plays well.

TRINCULO

I'm right behind you, Stephano. Are you coming monster?

They all exit.

ACT 3, SCENE 3

Enter ALONSO, SEBASTIAN, ANTONIO, GONZALO, ADRIAN,
FRANCISCO, *and others*

GONZALO
    (to ALONSO*)* By 'r lakin, I can go no further, sir.
    My old bones ache. Here's a maze trod indeed
    Through forthrights and meanders. By your patience,
    I needs must rest me.

ALONSO
                    Old lord, I cannot blame thee,
5   Who am myself attached with weariness
    To th' dulling of my spirits. Sit down and rest.
    Even here I will put off my hope and keep it
    No longer for my flatterer. He is drowned
    Whom thus we stray to find, and the sea mocks
10   Our frustrate search on land. Well, let him go.

ANTONIO
    (aside to SEBASTIAN*)* I am right glad that he's so out of hope.
    Do not for one repulse forego the purpose
    That you resolved t' effect.

SEBASTIAN
    (aside to ANTONIO*)*   The next advantage
    Will we take throughly.

ANTONIO
    (aside to SEBASTIAN*)*   Let it be tonight,
15   For now they are oppressed with travel. They
    Will not, nor cannot, use such vigilance
    As when they are fresh.

    Solemn and strange music
    Enter PROSPERO *on the top, invisible*

ACT 3, SCENE 3

ALONSO, SEBASTIAN, ANTONIO, GONZALO, ADRIAN,
FRANCISCO, *and others enter.*

GONZALO

I swear, I can't go any further, sir. My old bones are
tired. We're wandering in a maze. If you don't mind,
I need to rest a bit.

ALONSO

I can't blame you, old lord. I'm so tired myself that it's
bringing me down. Sit down and rest. I'm losing hope.
The one we're looking for is dead. We're searching on
land, but he's lost in the sea. We have to give up and let
him go.

ANTONIO

(speaking so that only SEBASTIAN *can hear)* I'm glad
he's so depressed. Don't back out of our plan just
because it didn't work the first time.

SEBASTIAN

(speaking so that only ANTONIO *can hear)* The next
chance we get, we'll do the deed.

ANTONIO

(speaking so that only SEBASTIAN *can hear)* Let's do it
tonight. The men are so tired from traveling that they
can't be as careful as they are when they're fresh.

Solemn and strange music is heard. PROSPERO *enters
above, invisible.*

SEBASTIAN
(aside to **ANTONIO***)* I say, tonight. No more.

ALONSO
What harmony is this? My good friends, hark!

GONZALO
20   Marvelous sweet music!

Enter several strange shapes, bringing in a banquet
They dance about it with gentle actions of salutations, and,
inviting the king and the others to eat, they depart

ALONSO
Give us kind keepers, heavens! What were these?

SEBASTIAN
A living drollery. Now I will believe
That there are unicorns, that in Arabia
There is one tree, the phoenix' throne, one phoenix
25   At this hour reigning there.

ANTONIO
                                        I'll believe both
And what does else want credit, come to me,
And I'll be sworn 'tis true. Travelers ne'er did lie,
Though fools at home condemn 'em.

GONZALO
                                        If in Naples
I should report this now, would they believe me?
30   If I should say, I saw such islanders—
For, certes, these are people of the island—
Who, though they are of monstrous shape, yet note,
Their manners are more gentle-kind than of
Our human generation you shall find
35   Many—nay, almost any.

PROSPERO
(aside)   Honest lord,
Thou hast said well, for some of you there present
Are worse than devils.

SEBASTIAN

(speaking so that only ANTONIO can hear) Yes, tonight. No more talking about this now.

ALONSO

What's that music? My friends, listen.

GONZALO

What marvelous music!

Several strange shapes enter, bringing in a banquet table and dancing around it with graceful, welcoming movements. After inviting the king and the others to eat, they leave.

ALONSO

Heaven help us! What were those things?

SEBASTIAN

A puppet show in real life. Now I'll believe that unicorns exist, and that there's a tree in Arabia where the phoenix lives.

ANTONIO

Me too. And anything else that's hard to believe, just ask me and I'll swear it's true. Travelers have never told lies, no matter what the fools at home accuse them of.

GONZALO

If I told them about this back in Naples, would they believe me? I'd tell them that I saw natives like these—since they must be natives—who are graceful and well-mannered even if they're monstrous to look at, kinder than most human beings you might find—kinder than almost any human.

PROSPERO

(to himself) My good lord, you're absolutely right, since some of you are worse than devils.

ALONSO
                                    I cannot too much muse
Such shapes, such gesture, and such sound, expressing,
Although they want the use of tongue, a kind
40   Of excellent dumb discourse.

PROSPERO
       (aside)   Praise in departing.

FRANCISCO
       They vanished strangely.

SEBASTIAN
                                    No matter, since
They have left their viands behind, for we have stomachs.
Will 't please you taste of what is here?

ALONSO
       Not I.

GONZALO
45   Faith, sir, you need not fear. When we were boys,
Who would believe that there were mountaineers
Dewlapped like bulls, whose throats had hanging at 'em
Wallets of flesh, or that there were such men
Whose heads stood in their breasts?—which now we find
50   Each putter-out of five for one will bring us
Good warrant of.

ALONSO
                                    I will stand to and feed,
Although my last. No matter, since I feel
The best is past. Brother, my lord the duke,
Stand to and do as we.

Thunder and lightning
Enter ARIEL, like a harpy, claps his wings upon the table, and,
with a quaint device, the banquet vanishes

ALONSO

I can't stop being amazed by these shapes, sounds, and gestures, which express, even without saying anything, a wonderful kind of silent language.

PROSPERO

(to himself) Time to go.

FRANCISCO

They vanished strangely.

SEBASTIAN

It's all right, since they left their food behind, and we're hungry. Would you like to taste the banquet?

ALONSO

Not me.

GONZALO

I assure you, sir, there's nothing to be afraid of. When we were boys, who'd believe that there were mountain people with rolls of skin around their necks, with their throats hanging down? Or that there were men with heads in their chests?—Nowadays travelers commonly report that these things exist.

ALONSO

I'll start eating, even if this is my last supper. It's all right, since the best part of my life was over anyway. Brother, Duke, please have some food.

Thunder and lightning. ARIEL *enters in the form of a harpy.* ARIEL *flaps his wings on the table, and the banquet vanishes from the table.*

A harpy is a mythological creature with a woman's face and breasts and the wings and claws of a bird. Shakespeare apparently intended to have Ariel appear together with two other harpies.

ARIEL
    (to ALONSO, ANTONIO, *and* SEBASTIAN*)*

55   You are three men of sin, whom Destiny,
    That hath to instrument this lower world
    And what is in 't, the never-surfeited sea
    Hath caused to belch up you—and on this island
    Where man doth not inhabit, you 'mongst men
60   Being most unfit to live. I have made you mad,
    And even with suchlike valor men hang and drown
    Their proper selves. *(some of the courtiers draw their swords)*
                 You fools, I and my fellows
    Are ministers of fate. The elements
    Of whom your swords are tempered may as well
65   Wound the loud winds or with bemocked-at stabs
    Kill the still-closing waters as diminish
    One dowl that's in my plume. My fellow ministers
    Are like invulnerable. If you could hurt,
    Your swords are now too massy for your strengths
70   And will not be uplifted. But remember—
    For that's my business to you—that you three
    From Milan did supplant good Prospero,
    Exposed unto the sea, which hath requit it,
    Him and his innocent child. For which foul deed
75   The powers—delaying, not forgetting—have
    Incensed the seas and shores, yea, all the creatures,
    Against your peace.—Thee of thy son, Alonso,
    They have bereft, and do pronounce by me
    Lingering perdition, worse than any death
80   Can be at once, shall step by step attend
    You and your ways; whose wraths to guard you from—
    Which here, in this most desolate isle, else falls
    Upon your heads—is nothing but hearts' sorrow
    And a clear life ensuing.

    ARIEL *vanishes in thunder*

ARIEL

(to ALONSO, ANTONIO, *and* SEBASTIAN*)* The three of you are sinners, and Destiny made the sea belch you up onto this island—where no men live, since none of you deserve to live. I've driven you crazy, and many mad people are driven to kill themselves in desperation. *(some of the courtiers draw their swords)* Listen, you fools, my fellow harpies and I carry out Fate's orders. Your swords are useless against us—you'd be more successful swinging them at the empty air, or stabbing at water, than trying to cut off even one of my feathers. My two companions are just as invulnerable as I am. Even if you had the power to hurt us, you'd find your swords far too heavy to lift. But remember— and it's my job to remind you of this—that in Milan the three of you stole Prospero's throne and threw him and his innocent child into the sea, which has now taken revenge on you. To punish you for this horrible crime, the higher powers—delaying their punishment, not forgetting about it—have stirred up the seas and all the creatures of earth against you.—They've taken your only son from you, Alonso, and they've ordered me to destroy you slowly, in a way worse than sudden death could ever be. I'll stay with you every step of your way. The only way to protect yourselves from the angry higher powers—which are ready to fall upon your head on this empty island—is for you to be sincerely sorry in your hearts for what you've done, and to live innocent lives from this time forward.

ARIEL *vanishes in thunder.*

*Then, to soft music enter the shapes again and dance, with
mocks and mows, and carrying out the table*

PROSPERO

85   *(aside)* Bravely the figure of this harpy hast thou
        Performed, my Ariel. A grace it had, devouring.
        Of my instruction hast thou nothing bated
        In what thou hadst to say.—So with good life
        And observation strange, my meaner ministers
90   Their several kinds have done. My high charms work
        And these mine enemies are all knit up
        In their distractions. They now are in my power,
        And in these fits I leave them while I visit
        Young Ferdinand, whom they suppose is drowned,
95   And his and mine loved darling.

                                        Exit PROSPERO *above*

GONZALO

        (to ALONSO*)* I' th' name of something holy, sir, why stand you
        In this strange stare?

ALONSO

                        Oh, it is monstrous, monstrous.
        Methought the billows spoke and told me of it,
        The winds did sing it to me, and the thunder,
100   That deep and dreadful organ pipe, pronounced
        The name of Prosper. It did bass my trespass.
        Therefore my son i' th' ooze is bedded, and
        I'll seek him deeper than e'er plummet sounded
        And with him there lie mudded.

                                        Exit ALONSO

The shapes enter again, accompanied by soft music. Dancing with mocking gestures and grimaces, they carry out the banquet table.

PROSPERO

(to himself) You've played the role of harpy very well, my Ariel. You were fierce but graceful. You said everything I told you to say.—In the same lifelike way, and with the same attention to detail, my lower-ranking servants have done what they were supposed to do. My magic powers are all in full swing, and my enemies are confused and running around in circles. They're under my control, and I'm keeping them in their crazy fits while I go visit Ferdinand, whom they think has drowned, and the young woman he and I both love.

PROSPERO *exits on a platform overhead.*

GONZALO

(to ALONSO*)* For the love of God, sir, why are you standing here staring into space like this?

ALONSO

Oh, it's horrible, horrible. I thought the clouds were talking to me, the winds were singing to me, and the thunder, like an awful organ pipe, roared Prospero's name. It sang about my crimes. Because of my crimes my son is dead on the ocean floor. I'll go join him there, going down deeper than any anchor ever sank, and lie with him dead in the mud.

ALONSO *exits.*

SEBASTIAN

But one fiend at a time,

105   I'll fight their legions o'er.

ANTONIO

I'll be thy second.

Exeunt SEBASTIAN *and* ANTONIO

GONZALO

All three of them are desperate. Their great guilt,
Like poison given to work a great time after,
Now 'gins to bite the spirits. I do beseech you
That are of suppler joints, follow them swiftly
110   And hinder them from what this ecstasy
May now provoke them to.

ADRIAN

Follow, I pray you.

Exeunt omnes

SEBASTIAN

I'll fight every one of these devils if I have to, one at a time.

ANTONIO

I'll back you up.

SEBASTIAN and ANTONIO exit.

GONZALO

All three of them are crazy with despair. Their guilt is finally starting to gnaw at them, like a slow-acting poison. Those of you who are young and active, I beg you to follow them and keep them from doing the crazy things their guilt might push them to do.

ADRIAN

Follow them, please.

They all exit.

ACT FOUR
SCENE 1

Enter PROSPERO, FERDINAND, *and* MIRANDA

PROSPERO
(to FERDINAND*)* If I have too austerely punished you,
Your compensation makes amends, for I
Have given you here a third of mine own life—
Or that for which I live—who once again
I tender to thy hand. All thy vexations
Were but my trials of thy love and thou
Hast strangely stood the test. Here, afore heaven,
I ratify this my rich gift. O Ferdinand,
Do not smile at me that I boast of her,
For thou shalt find she will outstrip all praise
And make it halt behind her.

FERDINAND
                                                I do believe it
Against an oracle.

PROSPERO
Then as my gift and thine own acquisition
Worthily purchased, take my daughter. But
If thou dost break her virgin knot before
All sanctimonious ceremonies may
With full and holy rite be ministered,
No sweet aspersion shall the heavens let fall
To make this contract grow, but barren hate,
Sour-eyed disdain, and discord shall bestrew
The union of your bed with weeds so loathly
That you shall hate it both. Therefore take heed,
As Hymen's lamps shall light you.

ACT FOUR
SCENE 1

PROSPERO, FERDINAND, *and* MIRANDA *enter.*

PROSPERO

(to FERDINAND*)* If I've punished you too harshly, I'm ready to make it up to you now, since I've given you a third of my life—everything I live for—my daughter Miranda. I put her in your hands. All the trouble I put you through was to test your love for her, and you've passed the test remarkably well. As heaven is my witness, I give you this valuable gift. Oh Ferdinand, don't smile at me for bragging about Miranda, for you'll see soon enough that she outshines any praise of her.

FERDINAND

An oracle is someone who delivers messages from the gods.

I'd believe it even if oracles told me differently.

PROSPERO

Then take my daughter, both as my gift to you and as something you have earned. But if you have sex with her before the marriage ceremony takes place, the heavens will not bless your relationship, but will overwhelm you with hate, contempt, and discord, and will poison your marriage bed so that you both grow to loathe it. So be careful, and make sure you respect the holy institution of marriage.

FERDINAND

As I hope

For quiet days, fair issue, and long life,

25 With such love as 'tis now, the murkiest den,

The most opportune place, the strong'st suggestion,

Our worser genius can shall never melt

Mine honor into lust to take away

The edge of that day's celebration

30 When I shall think, or Phoebus' steeds are foundered,

Or night kept chained below.

PROSPERO

Fairly spoke.

Sit then and talk with her. She is thine own.—

What, Ariel! My industrious servant, Ariel!

Enter ARIEL

ARIEL

What would my potent master? Here I am.

PROSPERO

35 Thou and thy meaner fellows your last service

Did worthily perform, and I must use you

In such another trick. Go bring the rabble,

O'er whom I give thee power, here to this place.

Incite them to quick motion, for I must

40 Bestow upon the eyes of this young couple

Some vanity of mine art. It is my promise,

And they expect it from me.

ARIEL

Presently?

PROSPERO

Ay, with a twink.

ARIEL

Before you can say "Come" and "Go,"

45 And breathe twice and cry "So, so!"

Each one, tripping on his toe,

FERDINAND

I want peace, good kids, and a long life. To protect the love I cherish, I won't be tempted by any opportunity to forget my honor and give in to lust. I refuse to give up the joys of my wedding day, when I'll be so eager for my first night of love that I'll wonder whether evening will ever come.

PROSPERO

You've said it well. So have a seat and talk to her. She's yours.—Come, Ariel! My trusty servant, Ariel!

ARIEL *enters.*

ARIEL

What does my powerful master wish for? I'm here.

PROSPERO

You and your fellow spirits did your last assignment well, and now I need your help again. Go bring them all here; I give you power over them. Make them act quickly. I have to give this young couple here a small display of my magic powers. I've promised them I would, and they're expecting it.

ARIEL

Right now?

PROSPERO

Yes, right away.

ARIEL

Before you can say "Come" and "Go,"
And breathe twice, and shout "So, so!"
Each one of your servants will rush here,

Will be here with mop and mow.
Do you love me, master, no?

PROSPERO
Dearly my delicate Ariel. Do not approach
50   Till thou dost hear me call.

ARIEL
                              Well, I conceive.

Exit ARIEL

PROSPERO
(to FERDINAND*)* Look thou be true. Do not give dalliance
Too much the rein. The strongest oaths are straw
To th' fire i' th' blood. Be more abstemious,
Or else, goodnight your vow.

FERDINAND
                              I warrant you, sir,
55   The white cold virgin snow upon my heart
Abates the ardor of my liver.

PROSPERO
                    Well.—
Now come, my Ariel! Bring a corollary,
Rather than want a spirit. Appear and pertly!—

Soft music

No tongue. All eyes! Be silent.

Enter IRIS

IRIS
60   Ceres, most bounteous lady, thy rich leas
Of wheat, rye, barley, vetches, oats, and peas;
Thy turfy mountains, where live nibbling sheep,
And flat meads thatched with stover, them to keep;
Thy banks with pionèd and twillèd brims,

Tripping over his own toes, making funny faces.
Do you love me, master? No?

PROSPERO

I love you dearly, Ariel. Don't come near till you hear me call you.

ARIEL

All right, I understand.

ARIEL exits.

PROSPERO

(to FERDINAND) Make sure you behave honorably. Don't go too far with her. If you let yourself get stirred up, you'll forget your promise of good behavior. Calm yourself down or you'll forget your vow.

FERDINAND

I assure you, sir, the tender love I feel in my heart is stronger than the sexual passions stirring down below.

PROSPERO

Good.—Now come, Ariel! Better to have an extra servant on hand than be understaffed. Appear before me now quickly—

Soft music plays.

No talking. Just watch! Be quiet.

IRIS enters.

IRIS

I am the rainbow-bearing messenger sent by my mistress Juno—the Queen of the Sky. I have come to announce that Juno has asked you, Ceres, goddess of the fields and the earth, to leave your rich farms of wheat, rye, barley, oats, and peas, the hills where the

65 Which spongy April at thy hest betrims
To make cold nymphs chaste crowns; and thy broom groves,
Whose shadow the dismissèd bachelor loves,
Being lass-lorn; thy pole-clipped vineyard;
And thy sea-marge, sterile and rocky hard,
70 Where thou thyself dost air—the Queen o' th' Sky,
Whose watery arch and messenger am I,
Bids thee leave these, and with her sovereign grace,

JUNO *descends above*

Here on this grass plot, in this very place,
To come and sport. Her peacocks fly amain.
75 Approach, rich Ceres, her to entertain.

Enter CERES

CERES
Hail, many-colored messenger, that ne'er
Dost disobey the wife of Jupiter;
Who with thy saffron wings upon my flowers
Diffusest honey drops, refreshing showers;
80 And with each end of thy blue bow dost crown
My bosky acres and my unshrubbed down,
Rich scarf to my proud earth. Why hath thy queen
Summoned me hither to this short-grassed green?

IRIS
A contract of true love to celebrate,
85 And some donation freely to estate
On the blessed lovers.

CERES
                                        Tell me, heavenly bow,
If Venus or her son, as thou dost know,

sheep nibble, the furrows that April covers with flowers for nymphs to make crowns with. You must leave the groves where the disappointed bachelor lurks, rejected by his love, and the well-pruned vineyards, and the rocky seashore.

JUNO *enters above the stage and slowly begins to descend.*

You must leave these places and hurry here to this grassy spot, to entertain Juno.

CERES *enters.*

CERES

Greetings to you, rainbow messenger, who never disobeys Juno, wife of Jupiter; with your golden wings you sprinkle dewdrops and refreshing showers on my flowers, and arch your colored bow over my wooded fields and grassy meadows, like a beautiful scarf to decorate my earth. Why has your queen, Juno, called me here to this grassy spot?

IRIS

To celebrate a marriage of true love, and give a gift to the lovers.

CERES

Tell me, rainbow, do you know if either Venus, the goddess of love, or her son, Cupid, is accompanying

Do now attend the queen? Since they did plot
The means that dusky Dis my daughter got,
90   Her and her blind boy's scandaled company
I have forsworn.

IRIS
                              Of her society
Be not afraid. I met her deity
Cutting the clouds towards Paphos, and her son
Dove-drawn with her. Here thought they to have done
95   Some wanton charm upon this man and maid,
Whose vows are that no bed-right shall be paid
Till Hymen's torch be lighted—but in vain.
Mars's hot minion is returned again.
Her waspish-headed son has broke his arrows,
100   Swears he will shoot no more, but play with sparrows
And be a boy right out.

CERES
                              Highest queen of state,
Great Juno, comes. I know her by her gait.

JUNO descends to the stage

JUNO
How does my bounteous sister? Go with me
To bless this twain that they may prosperous be,
105   And honored in their issue.

They sing

JUNO
(*sings*)
          Honor, riches, marriage, blessing,
          Long continuance, and increasing,
          Hourly joys be still upon you.
          Juno sings her blessings on you.

Queen Juno? Ever since Venus and her blind son plotted a way for the god of the underworld to steal my daughter away for half the year, I swore I'd never speak to them again.

IRIS

Don't be afraid of her company. I met Venus as she was with her son on her way to her home on Paphos, in a carriage pulled by doves. They were planning to pull a mischievous trick on Ferdinand and Miranda, who have sworn not to sleep together till their wedding day. But their trick failed. Venus went home again, and her little son broke all his arrows, swearing he'll never shoot them again, but play with birds like other little boys.

CERES

Great Queen Juno is coming. I know her by her walk.

JUNO *comes down to the stage.*

JUNO

How is my generous sister? Come help me bless this couple, so they will be prosperous and have many children.

They sing.

JUNO

(*singing*)
>May honor, riches, marriage blessings,
>Long life, and unending joys come to you.
>Juno sings her blessings onto you.

CERES
(sings)

110   Earth's increase, foison plenty,
             Barns and garners never empty,
             Vines and clustering bunches growing,
             Plants with goodly burden bowing—
             Spring come to you at the farthest
115   In the very end of harvest.
             Scarcity and want shall shun you.
             Ceres' blessing so is on you.

FERDINAND
             This is a most majestic vision, and
             Harmonious charmingly. May I be bold
120   To think these spirits?

PROSPERO
                                        Spirits, which by mine art
             I have from their confines called to enact
             My present fancies.

FERDINAND
                                   Let me live here ever.
             So rare a wondered father and a wife
             Makes this place paradise.

             JUNO and CERES whisper, and send IRIS on employment

PROSPERO
                                        Sweet now, silence.
125   Juno and Ceres whisper seriously.
             There's something else to do. Hush and be mute,
             Or else our spell is marred.

IRIS
             You nymphs, called naiads of the windring brooks,
             With your sedged crowns and ever-harmless looks,
130   Leave your crisp channels and on this green land
             Answer your summons, Juno does command.

CERES

> *(singing)*
>> Growing crops and large harvests,
>> Barns and silos full of grain,
>> Vines heavy with clustered grapes,
>> Plants straining under their fruit—
>> May spring follow directly autumn's harvest,
>> With none of winter's hardships to endure,
>> You will have plenty and want nothing,
>> Ceres's blessings on you.

FERDINAND

> This is a majestic and harmonious vision. Are these spirits we see before us?

PROSPERO

> Yes, they're spirits that I've called out of their prisons to perform my whims.

FERDINAND

> Let me live here forever. Such a wonderful father-in-law and wife make this place a paradise.

JUNO *and* CERES *whisper, then send* IRIS *on a mission.*

PROSPERO

> Now be quiet. Juno and Ceres are whispering about something serious. There's something else to be done. Be silent, or else my magic spell will be broken.

IRIS

> You nymphs who live in the wandering brooks, with seaweed crowns and innocent looks, step out of the water and come join us here on this grassy field. Juno

Come, temperate nymphs, and help to celebrate
A contract of true love. Be not too late.

Enter certain nymphs

You sunburnt sicklemen of August weary,
135   Come hither from the furrow and be merry.
Make holiday. Your rye-straw hats put on,
And these fresh nymphs encounter every one
In country footing.

Enter certain reapers, properly habited
They join with the nymphs in a graceful dance towards the end
whereof PROSPERO *starts suddenly and speaks.*

PROSPERO
I had forgot that foul conspiracy
140   Of the beast Caliban and his confederates
Against my life. The minute of their plot
Is almost come.—Well done. Avoid, no more!

To a strange, hollow, and confused noise, the spirits heavily
vanish

FERDINAND
(*to* MIRANDA) This is strange. Your father's in some passion
That works him strongly.

MIRANDA
                                          Never till this day
145   Saw I him touched with anger so distempered.

PROSPERO
(*to* FERDINAND) You do look, my son, in a moved sort,
As if you were dismayed. Be cheerful, sir.
Our revels now are ended. These our actors,
As I foretold you, were all spirits and
150   Are melted into air, into thin air.

orders you. Come, sweet nymphs, and help us celebrate the wedding of two true lovers. Don't be late.

Several NYMPHS *enter.*

Now, you tanned fieldworkers who are so tired of August's labors, get out of the dirt and come rejoice with us here. Put your straw hats on, have some fun, and dance with these young nymphs.

Several fieldworkers enter, dressed appropriately. They join the nymphs in a graceful dance. At the end PROSPERO *suddenly acts startled and speaks.*

PROSPERO

I almost forgot about Caliban's horrible conspiracy to kill me. The moment they planned to act is almost here. *(to the spirits)*—Good job. Leave now, no more!

The dancers vanish sadly to a strange, hollow, and confused noise.

FERDINAND

(to MIRANDA*)* This is strange. Something has really upset your father.

MIRANDA

I've never seen him like this. He's never been as angry and upset as he is now.

PROSPERO

(to FERDINAND*)* You look like something's bothering you. Cheer up. Our music-and-dance spectacle is over. These actors were all spirits, as I told you, and they've all melted into thin air. And just like the whole empty and ungrounded vision you've seen, with its

And like the baseless fabric of this vision,
The cloud-capped towers, the gorgeous palaces,
The solemn temples, the great globe itself—
Yea, all which it inherit—shall dissolve,
155   And like this insubstantial pageant faded,
Leave not a rack behind. We are such stuff
As dreams are made on, and our little life
Is rounded with a sleep. Sir, I am vexed.
Bear with my weakness. My old brain is troubled.
160   Be not disturbed with my infirmity.
If you be pleased, retire into my cell
And there repose. A turn or two I'll walk
To still my beating mind.

FERDINAND, MIRANDA
We wish your peace.

Exeunt FERDINAND *and* MIRANDA

PROSPERO
165   Come with a thought. I thank thee, Ariel. Come.

Enter ARIEL

ARIEL
Thy thoughts I cleave to. What's thy pleasure?
PROSPERO
                                                    Spirit,
We must prepare to meet with Caliban.
ARIEL
Ay, my commander. When I presented Ceres,
I thought to have told thee of it, but I feared
170   Lest I might anger thee.
PROSPERO
Say again, where didst thou leave these varlets?

towers topped with clouds, its gorgeous palaces, solemn temples, the world itself—and everyone living in it—which will dissolve just as this illusory pageant has dissolved, leaving not even a wisp of cloud behind. We are all made of dreams, and our life stretches from sleep before birth to sleep after death. Sir, I'm upset. Please put up with my weakness. My old brain is troubled. Don't be disturbed by my illness. If you like, you can rest a while in my room. I'll go for a short walk to calm down my feverish mind.

FERDINAND, MIRANDA

We hope you feel better and find some peace.

They exit.

PROSPERO

Come, Ariel—I summon you with a thought. Thank you, Ariel. Come.

ARIEL *enters.*

ARIEL

I obey all your thoughts. What do you wish?

PROSPERO

Spirit, we have to get ready to meet with Caliban.

ARIEL

Yes, my master. When I was putting on the Ceres show, I thought of reminding you about Caliban, but I was afraid of upsetting you.

PROSPERO

Tell me again, where did you leave those lowlifes?

ARIEL
I told you, sir, they were red-hot with drinking,
So full of valor that they smote the air
For breathing in their faces, beat the ground
175   For kissing of their feet—yet always bending
Towards their project. Then I beat my tabor,
At which, like unbacked colts, they pricked their ears,
Advanced their eyelids, lifted up their noses
As they smelt music. So I charmed their ears
180   That, calflike, they my lowing followed through
Toothed briers, sharp furzes, pricking gorse, and thorns,
Which entered their frail shins. At last I left them
I' th' filthy-mantled pool beyond your cell,
There dancing up to th' chins, that the foul lake
185   O'erstunk their feet.

PROSPERO
                              This was well done, my bird.
Thy shape invisible retain thou still.
The trumpery in my house, go bring it hither
For stale to catch these thieves.

ARIEL
                                        I go, I go.

                                        Exit ARIEL

PROSPERO
A devil, a born devil on whose nature
190   Nurture can never stick, on whom my pains,
Humanely taken, all, all lost, quite lost.
And as with age his body uglier grows,
So his mind cankers. I will plague them all,
Even to roaring.

Enter ARIEL, *loaden with glistering apparel, etc.*

195   Come, hang them on this line.

ARIEL

> I told you, sir, they were totally drunk, so puffed up
> with courage that they were getting angry at the air for
> blowing in their faces, and beating the ground for
> touching their feet—yet even when drunk, they kept
> their plan firmly in mind. Then I beat my drum, at
> which point they pricked up their ears and opened
> their eyes, looking around for the source of my music.
> I enchanted them so thoroughly that they followed me
> through thorn bushes and prickly shrubs that tore up
> their shins. In the end I left them standing in the
> smelly pond behind your room, with the stinking
> water covering them up to their chins.

PROSPERO

> Good job, my little one. Stay invisible. Bring the fancy
> clothes out of my house, to use as bait to catch these
> thieves.

ARIEL

> I'm going, I'm going.

ARIEL *exits.*

PROSPERO

> He's a devil, a born devil, who can never be trained.
> All my attempts to help him, undertaken with the best
> intentions, have been wasted. As his body grows
> uglier with age, his mind rots away as well. I'll tor-
> ment them all till they roar with pain.

ARIEL *enters, loaded with sparkling clothes.*

> Here, hang them on this clothesline.

Enter CALIBAN, STEPHANO, *and* TRINCULO, *all wet*

CALIBAN
Pray you, tread softly, that the blind mole may not hear a
foot fall. We now are near his cell.

STEPHANO
Monster, your fairy, which you say is a harmless fairy, has
done little better than played the jack with us.

TRINCULO
200   Monster, I do smell all horse piss, at which my nose is in
great indignation.

STEPHANO
So is mine.—Do you hear, monster? If I should take a
displeasure against you, look you—

TRINCULO
Thou wert but a lost monster.

CALIBAN
205   Good my lord, give me thy favor still.
Be patient, for the prize I'll bring thee to
Shall hoodwink this mischance. Therefore speak softly.
All's hushed as midnight yet.

TRINCULO
Ay, but to lose our bottles in the pool—

STEPHANO
210   There is not only disgrace and dishonor in that, monster,
but an infinite loss.

TRINCULO
That's more to me than my wetting. Yet this is your
harmless fairy, monster.

STEPHANO
I will fetch off my bottle, though I be o'er ears for my labor.

CALIBAN, STEPHANO, *and* TRINCULO *enter all wet.*

CALIBAN

Please walk softly, so not even a mole hears us approach. We're near his room now.

STEPHANO

Hey monster, the spirit you've been talking about, the one you call harmless, has been playing tricks on us.

TRINCULO

Monster, I smell like horse piss, which is making my nose pretty upset.

STEPHANO

Mine too.—Are you listening, monster? If I decide to get angry at you, just watch out—

TRINCULO

You'd be done for then, monster.

CALIBAN

My good lord, I still need you to like me. Be patient, because the prize I'm leading you to will make you forget how smelly you are now. So be quiet. It's as silent as a graveyard here.

TRINCULO

All right, but I can't get over how we lost our wine bottles in the pond—

STEPHANO

Yes, monster, it's worse than the disgrace of getting drenched and smelly. We lost more than our honor when we lost our wine.

TRINCULO

That upsets me much more than getting wet. And you called the fairy creature harmless, monster.

STEPHANO

I'll get my bottle back if it's the last thing I do.

CALIBAN

215   Prithee, my king, be quiet. Seest thou here,
         This is the mouth o' th' cell. No noise, and enter.
         Do that good mischief which may make this island
         Thine own for ever, and I, thy Caliban,
         For aye thy foot-licker.

STEPHANO

220   Give me thy hand. I do begin to have bloody thoughts.

TRINCULO

         (seeing the apparel)
         O King Stephano! O peer, O worthy Stephano, look what a
         wardrobe here is for thee!

CALIBAN

         Let it alone, thou fool. It is but trash.

TRINCULO

         Oh, ho, monster, we know what belongs to a frippery.—
225   *(puts on a gown)* O King Stephano!

STEPHANO

         Put off that gown, Trinculo. By this hand, I'll have
         that gown.

TRINCULO

         Thy grace shall have it.

CALIBAN

         The dropsy drown this fool! What do you mean
230   To dote thus on such luggage? Let's alone,
         And do the murder first. If he awake,
         From toe to crown he'll fill our skins with pinches,
         Make us strange stuff.

STEPHANO

         Be you quiet, monster.—Mistress line, is not this my
235   jerkin? Now is the jerkin under the line.—Now, jerkin, you
         are like to lose your hair and prove a bald jerkin.

CALIBAN

Please, my king, be quiet. Look here, this is the entrance to his room. Be silent and go in. Do the deed that will make this island yours forever, and will make me, Caliban, your worshipful foot-licker.

STEPHANO

Give me your hand. I'm starting to feel murderous urges.

TRINCULO

(seeing the clothes) Oh, King Stephano! Worthy Stephano, look at the fabulous wardrobe waiting for you here!

CALIBAN

Leave it alone, you fool. It's worthless.

TRINCULO

Oh, monster, we know secondhand clothes when we see them.—*(he puts on one of the gowns)* Oh, King Stephano!

STEPHANO

Take off that gown, Trinculo. I swear that gown's for me.

TRINCULO

You can have it then, your highness.

CALIBAN

To hell with this idiot! Why are you going crazy over these trashy clothes? Leave them alone, and do the murder first. If he wakes up before we kill him, he'll never stop punishing us.

STEPHANO

Stephano makes an elaborate (and untranslatable) pun about the shirt being like a sailor who goes to the tropics and gets a venereal disease.

Shut up, monster.—Madame tree, is this jacket for me? Thank you kindly. The tree's lost its jacket. *(he takes a jacket hanging on the tree)*—Now the jacket might lose its fur trim and become a bald jacket.

TRINCULO
> Do, do. We steal by line and level, an 't like your grace.

STEPHANO
> I thank thee for that jest. Here's a garment for 't. Wit shall
> not go unrewarded while I am king of this country. "Steal
> by line and level" is an excellent pass of pate. There's
> another garment for 't.

TRINCULO
> Monster, come, put some lime upon your fingers, and away
> with the rest.

CALIBAN
> I will have none on 't. We shall lose our time,
> And all be turned to barnacles or to apes
> With foreheads villainous low.

STEPHANO
> Monster, lay to your fingers. Help to bear this away where
> my hogshead of wine is, or I'll turn you out of my kingdom.
> Go to, carry this.

TRINCULO
> And this.

STEPHANO
> Ay, and this.

> *A noise of hunters heard*
> *Enter divers spirits, in shape of dogs and hounds, hunting*
> *them about,* PROSPERO *and* ARIEL *setting them on*

PROSPERO
> Hey, Mountain, hey!

ARIEL
> Silver. There it goes, Silver!

TRINCULO

Go ahead, take it. We're stealing things the right way here.

STEPHANO

Thank you for that joke. Here, I'll give you some clothes to show my gratitude. As king of this country I like to reward wit when I hear it. "Stealing things the right way" is a great line. Here's another jacket to say thanks.

TRINCULO

Come here, monster, put some glue on your fingers, and carry away the rest of these clothes for us.

CALIBAN

I won't have any of this. We're wasting our time. We'll miss our chance and be turned into geese or apes with low foreheads.

STEPHANO

Monster, use your fingers. Help us carry these clothes to where my barrel of wine is hidden, or I'll kick you out of my kingdom. Go on, take them.

TRINCULO

Take these too.

STEPHANO

Yes, and these.

A noise of hunters is heard. Various spirits enter disguised as dogs and hounds, chasing STEPHANO, TRINCULO, *and* CALIBAN *around.* PROSPERO *and* ARIEL *follow them, urging the dogs on.*

PROSPERO

Hey, Mountain, hey!

ARIEL

Silver. There they go, Silver!

PROSPERO
Fury, Fury!—There, Tyrant, there. Hark, hark!

Spirits drive out CALIBAN, STEPHANO, *and* TRINCULO

Go charge my goblins that they grind their joints
255   With dry convulsions, shorten up their sinews
With agèd cramps, and more pinch-spotted make them
Than pard or cat o' mountain.

ARIEL
                                        Hark, they roar.

PROSPERO
Let them be hunted soundly. At this hour
Lie at my mercy all mine enemies.
260   Shortly shall all my labors end, and thou
Shalt have the air at freedom. For a little
Follow, and do me service.

                                                        Exeunt

PROSPERO

Fury, Fury!—Get over there, Tyrant, there. Listen, listen!

CALIBAN, STEPHANO, *and* TRINCULO *are chased away.*

Ariel, go order my goblin servants to make these fellows' bones ache, give them muscle cramps all over, and give them more bruises than leopards have spots.

ARIEL

Listen they're howling.

PROSPERO

Hunt them down. Now all my enemies are at my mercy. Soon all my work will be done, and you'll be free. Just obey me a little bit longer.

They exit.

ACT FIVE
SCENE 1

Enter PROSPERO *in his magic robes and* ARIEL

PROSPERO
Now does my project gather to a head.
My charms crack not, my spirits obey, and time
Goes upright with his carriage. How's the day?

ARIEL
On the sixth hour, at which time, my lord,
5   You said our work should cease.

PROSPERO
                I did say so
When first I raised the tempest. Say, my spirit,
How fares the king and 's followers?

ARIEL
                    Confined together
In the same fashion as you gave in charge,
Just as you left them, all prisoners, sir,
10   In the line grove which weather-fends your cell.
They cannot budge till your release. The king,
His brother, and yours, abide all three distracted,
And the remainder mourning over them,
Brimful of sorrow and dismay. But chiefly
15   Him that you termed, sir, "the good old Lord Gonzalo,"
His tears run down his beard like winter's drops
From eaves of reeds. Your charm so strongly works 'em
That if you now beheld them, your affections
Would become tender.

PROSPERO
               Dost thou think so, spirit?

ARIEL
20   Mine would, sir, were I human.

ACT FIVE
SCENE 1

PROSPERO *enters in his magic robes, with* ARIEL.

PROSPERO

My plans are almost at their climax. My spells are working well, my spirits are obeying me, and everything is right on schedule. What time is it?

ARIEL

It's after six o'clock, my lord, when you said our work would be finished.

PROSPERO

That's what I said when I first conjured the tempest. Tell me, spirit, how's the king and his entourage?

ARIEL

All cooped up together, just as you ordered, all imprisoned in the grove of linden trees that protects your room from bad weather. They can't move till you release them. The king, his brother, and your brother are all waiting there in a crazed state of mind, and the rest are grieving over them, sad and astonished. "Good old lord Gonzalo," as you call him, is saddest of all, with tears running down his beard. Your magic spell has such an effect on them that if you saw them now, you'd feel sorry for them.

PROSPERO

Do you think so, spirit?

ARIEL

I'd feel sorry for them, if I were human.

PROSPERO

                                        And mine shall.
Hast thou, which art but air, a touch, a feeling
Of their afflictions, and shall not myself,
One of their kind, that relish all as sharply
Passion as they, be kindlier moved than thou art?
25   Though with their high wrongs I am struck to th' quick,
Yet with my nobler reason 'gainst my fury
Do I take part. The rarer action is
In virtue than in vengeance. They being penitent,
The sole drift of my purpose doth extend
30   Not a frown further. Go release them, Ariel.
My charms I'll break, their senses I'll restore,
And they shall be themselves.

ARIEL

                                        I'll fetch them, sir.

                                        Exit **ARIEL**

PROSPERO
(tracing a circle on the ground)
Ye elves of hills, brooks, standing lakes, and groves,
And ye that on the sands with printless foot
35   Do chase the ebbing Neptune and do fly him
When he comes back; you demi-puppets that
By moonshine do the green sour ringlets make,
Whereof the ewe not bites; and you whose pastime
Is to make midnight mushrooms, that rejoice
40   To hear the solemn curfew; by whose aid,
Weak masters though ye be, I have bedimmed
The noontide sun, called forth the mutinous winds,
And 'twixt the green sea and the azured vault
Set roaring war—to th' dread rattling thunder
45   Have I given fire, and rifted Jove's stout oak

PROSPERO

I will too. You're made of air, so if even you feel sorry
for them, imagine the pity that I'll feel, being one of
their own human race. I suffer pain just as much as
they do, so I'll sympathize far more than you. Though
I'm indignant about their evil deeds, I'll go with my
nobler instincts, which tell me to feel some compassion for them. It's better to act virtuously rather than
vengefully. Now that they're sorry, I don't want anything more. Go release them, Ariel. I'll break my
spells and bring them back to their senses, and they'll
feel like themselves again.

ARIEL

I'll go get them, sir.

ARIEL *exits.*

PROSPERO

(drawing a large circle on the stage with his staff) I've
darkened the noontime sun with the aid of you elves
who live in the hills and brooks and groves, and you
who chase the sea on the beach without leaving foot-
prints in the sand, and run away when the waves come
back; and you who make toadstools while the moon
shines; who make mushrooms as a hobby after the
evening bell has rung. With your help I've called up
the angry winds, and set the green sea and blue sky at
war with each other. I've given lightning to the thun-
derclouds, and burned up Jupiter's beloved oak.

With his own bolt;
                  the strong-based promontory
Have I made shake, and by the spurs plucked up
The pine and cedar; graves at my command
Have waked their sleepers, oped, and let 'em forth
50   By my so potent art. But this rough magic
I here abjure, and when I have required
Some heavenly music, which even now I do,
To work mine end upon their senses that
This airy charm is for, I'll break my staff,
55   Bury it certain fathoms in the earth,
And deeper than did ever plummet sound
I'll drown my book.

Solemn music
Enter ARIEL *before,*
Then ALONSO, *with a frantic gesture, attended by* GONZALO;
SEBASTIAN *and* ANTONIO *in like manner, attended by* ADRIAN
and FRANCISCO—*they all enter the circle which* PROSPERO
had made, and there stand charmed; which PROSPERO
observing, speaks:

A solemn air and the best comforter
To an unsettled fancy cure thy brains,
60   Now useless, boiled within thy skull.—There stand,
For you are spell-stopped.—
(to GONZALO*)* Holy Gonzalo, honorable man,
Mine eyes, ev'n sociable to the show of thine,
Fall fellowly drops.
(aside)   The charm dissolves apace,
65   And as the morning steals upon the night,
Melting the darkness, so their rising senses
Begin to chase the ignorant fumes that mantle
Their clearer reason.—
(to GONZALO*)*   O good Gonzalo,
My true preserver and a loyal sir

With his own lightning bolts; I've shaken up the sturdy cliffs and uprooted pines and cedars; I've opened up graves and awakened the corpses sleeping in them, letting them out with my powerful magic. But I surrender all this magic now, when I've summoned some heavenly music to cast a spell, as I'm doing now, I'll break my staff and bury it far underground, and throw my book of magic spells deeper into the sea than any anchor ever sank.

Solemn music plays.

ARIEL *enters, followed by* ALONSO *gesturing frantically, accompanied by* GONZALO. SEBASTIAN *and* ANTONIO *enter in the same way, accompanied by* ADRIAN *and* FRANCISCO. *They all enter the circle that* PROSPERO *has drawn and stand there under a spell.* PROSPERO, *watching all of this, speaks, though the others do not hear him.*

Let this solemn melody comfort your fevered minds, which are now useless, seething inside your skulls.— All of you stand there in my spell.—*(to* GONZALO*)* Good Gonzalo, you honorable man, my eyes weep for you, since I feel what you must feel now. *(to himself)* The spell is breaking gradually, and just as dawn creeps in and melts away the darkness, they will slowly return to their senses.—*(to* GONZALO*)* Oh, my dear Gonzalo, you're my savior and loyal to your lord, I'll reward you fully, not just with praise but with actions too.—

70   To him you follow'st, I will pay thy graces
        Home both in word and deed.—
        (*to* ALONSO)   Most cruelly
        Didst thou, Alonso, use me and my daughter.
        Thy brother was a furtherer in the act.—
        (*to* SEBASTIAN) Thou art pinched for 't now, Sebastian.—
75   (*to* ANTONIO) Flesh and blood,
        You brother mine, that entertained ambition,
        Expelled remorse and nature, whom, with Sebastian,
        Whose inward pinches therefore are most strong,
        Would here have killed your king—I do forgive thee,
80   Unnatural though thou art.
        (*aside*)   Their understanding
        Begins to swell, and the approaching tide
        Will shortly fill the reasonable shore
        That now lies foul and muddy. Not one of them
        That yet looks on me, or would know me.—
        (*to* ARIEL)   Ariel,
85   Fetch me the hat and rapier in my cell.
        I will discase me, and myself present
        As I was sometime Milan. Quickly, spirit.
        Thou shalt ere long be free.

ARIEL
        (*sings and helps to attire* PROSPERO)
            Where the bee sucks, there suck I.
90   *In a cowslip's bell I lie.*
            There I couch when owls do cry.
            On the bat's back I do fly
            After summer merrily.
            Merrily, merrily shall I live now
95   *Under the blossom that hangs on the bough.*

PROSPERO
        Why, that's my dainty Ariel. I shall miss thee,
        But yet thou shalt have freedom.—So, so, so.—
        To the king's ship, invisible as thou art.
        There shalt thou find the mariners asleep

(to ALONSO*)* You, Alonso, manipulated me and my daughter cruelly, and your brother helped you.—*(to* SEBASTIAN*)* You're paying the price for it now, Sebastian.—*(to* ANTONIO*)* My brother, you were so greedy for power that you forgot natural compassion and our bond as brothers, and were ready to kill your king—I forgive you, though you're a monster.—*(to himself)* Look at them, they're starting to understand. Soon their confused minds will clear up. But at this point not a single one of them recognizes me.—*(to* ARIEL*)* Ariel, get me my hat and sword from my room. I'll take off the clothes I'm wearing now, and put on the ones I used to wear in Milan.—Soon, spirit, you'll be free.

ARIEL

(he sings and helps PROSPERO *dress)*
  Where the bee drinks, I drink dew.
  I lie in the cup of a cowslip flower.
  I sleep there when the owls hoot.
  I fly on a bat's back,
  following the summer around the globe.
  Happily, happily I will live now
  Under the blossom that hangs on the bough.

PROSPERO

Why, that's my dainty Ariel singing now. I'll miss you, Ariel, but you'll be free.—Yes, you will, yes.—Go to the king's ship in your invisible state. There

100   Under the hatches. The Master and the Boatswain
        Being awake, enforce them to this place,
        And presently, I prithee.

ARIEL
        I drink the air before me, and return
        Or ere your pulse twice beat.

Exit ARIEL

GONZALO
105   All torment, trouble, wonder, and amazement
        Inhabits here. Some heavenly power guide us
        Out of this fearful country!

PROSPERO
        (to ALONSO*)*   Behold, sir King,
        The wrongèd Duke of Milan, Prospero.
        For more assurance that a living prince
110   Does now speak to thee, I embrace thy body.
        And to thee and thy company I bid
        A hearty welcome. *(embraces* ALONSO*)*

ALONSO
                                   Whe'er thou beest he or no,
        Or some enchanted trifle to abuse me,
        As late I have been, I not know. Thy pulse
115   Beats as of flesh and blood. And since I saw thee,
        Th' affliction of my mind amends, with which
        I fear a madness held me. This must crave—
        An if this be at all—a most strange story.
        Thy dukedom I resign and do entreat
120   Thou pardon me my wrongs. But how should Prospero
        Be living and be here?

PROSPERO
        (to GONZALO*)*   First, noble friend,
        Let me embrace thine age, whose honor cannot
        Be measured or confined.

you'll find the sailors asleep below deck. Find the Master and Boatswain, who will be awake, and bring them here right away, please.

ARIEL

I'll go so fast I'll burn up the air, and come back in two heartbeats.

ARIEL exits.

GONZALO

This place is full of trouble, torments, and amazements. Please come, heavenly powers, and guide us out of this godforsaken country!

PROSPERO

(to ALONSO) Your Highness, you see before you the Duke of Milan, Prospero, who's been wronged. I'll embrace you now so you will know it's really me, a living prince, talking to you. I heartily welcome you and your entourage here. *(he embraces ALONSO)*

ALONSO

Whether you're really him or whether this is some magic trick like I was recently subjected to, I don't know. Your heart beats like you were real, and ever since I saw you, I feel my mind becoming sane again, released from its earlier insanity. There must be a strange explanation for this—if it's true. I surrender your dukedom and beg you to forgive me all my crimes. But how is it possible that Prospero's alive and well and living on this island?

PROSPERO

(to GONZALO) First, my noble old friend, let me embrace you, who are more honorable than I can say.

GONZALO
                                        Whether this be
Or be not, I'll not swear.

PROSPERO
                                        You do yet taste
125   Some subtleties o' th' isle, that will not let you
Believe things certain. Welcome, my friends all.
(aside to **SEBASTIAN** *and* **ANTONIO***)*
But you, my brace of lords, were I so minded,
I here could pluck his highness' frown upon you
And justify you traitors. At this time
130   I will tell no tales.

SEBASTIAN
                                        The devil speaks in him.

PROSPERO
                                        No.— *(to* **ANTONIO***)*
For you, most wicked sir, whom to call brother
Would even infect my mouth, I do forgive
Thy rankest fault, all of them, and require
My dukedom of thee, which perforce, I know,
135   Thou must restore.

ALONSO
                                        If thou beest Prospero,
Give us particulars of thy preservation,
How thou hast met us here, whom three hours since
Were wracked upon this shore, where I have lost—
How sharp the point of this remembrance is!
140   My dear son Ferdinand.

PROSPERO
                                        I am woe for 't, sir.

ALONSO
Irreparable is the loss, and patience
Says it is past her cure.

GONZALO

I won't bet on whether or not any of this is real.

PROSPERO

You're still experiencing some of the little quirks of this island, which makes so many things seem uncertain. Welcome, my friends. *(speaking so that only* SEBASTIAN *and* ANTONIO *can hear)* But you two lords, if I felt like it, I could turn you in as the traitors you are. But as for now, I won't say a word.

SEBASTIAN

It's the devil speaking through him.

PROSPERO

No.—*(to* ANTONIO*)* As for you, you evil man that I can't even call brother, I forgive you for even your worst sin, all your sins. I demand my dukedom back from you, which I know you have to give me.

ALONSO

If you're Prospero, give us the details of how you were saved, how you met us here, when we were just shipwrecked here three hours ago, when I lost—How painful the memory is!—my dear son Ferdinand

PROSPERO

I'm sorry about that, sir.

ALONSO

No one can undo this loss of mine, and trying to endure it patiently doesn't help.

PROSPERO
                              I rather think
You have not sought her help, of whose soft grace
For the like loss I have her sovereign aid,
And rest myself content.

ALONSO
                              You the like loss?

PROSPERO
As great to me as late. And supportable
To make the dear loss have I means much weaker
Than you may call to comfort you, for I
Have lost my daughter.

ALONSO
                              A daughter?
O heavens, that they were living both in Naples,
The king and queen there! That they were, I wish
Myself were mudded in that oozy bed
Where my son lies.—When did you lose your daughter?

PROSPERO
In this last tempest. I perceive these lords
At this encounter do so much admire
That they devour their reason and scarce think
Their eyes do offices of truth, their words
Are natural breath.—But howsoev'r you have
Been justled from your senses, know for certain
That I am Prospero and that very duke
Which was thrust forth of Milan, who most strangely
Upon this shore where you were wracked, was landed,
To be the lord on 't.

PROSPERO

I don't think you've tried to endure it. Being patient has helped me a lot, for I have suffered a loss similar to yours.

ALONSO

You suffered a loss like mine?

PROSPERO

Yes, just as great and just as recent. And I have much less to comfort me than you do, since I've lost my daughter.

ALONSO

A daughter? Oh God, I wish the two of them were alive and living in Naples, as king and queen! I'd give up my life and take my son's place in the mud on the ocean floor if I could see them alive in Naples.— When did you lose your daughter?

PROSPERO

In this recent storm. These lords seem so astonished that they've lost their use of reason and can hardly believe what they see with their own eyes.—But whatever the reason for your losing your senses, you can know for sure that I'm Prospero, that same duke who was kicked out of Milan and landed on this same island where you landed, and became the lord of it. No more of this story now, for it takes days to tell, not just a chat over breakfast or during this first meeting of ours.

                                        No more yet of this,
            For 'tis a chronicle of day by day,
165   Not a relation for a breakfast, nor
            Befitting this first meeting.
            (to ALONSO*)*   Welcome, sir.
            This cell's my court. Here have I few attendants
            And subjects none abroad. Pray you, look in.
            My dukedom since you have given me again,
170   I will requite you with as good a thing,
            At least bring forth a wonder to content ye
            As much as me my dukedom.

            Here PROSPERO *uncovers* FERDINAND *and* MIRANDA *playing
            at chess*

MIRANDA
            (to FERDINAND*)* Sweet lord, you play me false.

FERDINAND
            No, my dearest love,
175   I would not for the world.

MIRANDA
            Yes, for a score of kingdoms you should wrangle,
            And I would call it fair play.

ALONSO
                                        If this prove
            A vision of the Island, one dear son
            Shall I twice lose.

SEBASTIAN
                                A most high miracle!

FERDINAND
            (seeing ALONSO *and kneeling)*
180   Though the seas threaten, they are merciful.
            I have cursed them without cause.

(to ALONSO*)* Welcome, sir. This room's my royal court. I have hardly any servants and no subjects outside this room. Please, have a look. Since you've given my dukedom back to me, I'll give you something equally nice, or at least I'll give you an amazement to satisfy you as much as my dukedom satisfies me.

PROSPERO *draws a curtain to reveal* FERDINAND *and* MIRANDA *playing chess.*

MIRANDA

(to FERDINAND*)* My sweet lord, you're cheating.

FERDINAND

No, my dearest love, I wouldn't cheat you for the whole world.

MIRANDA

Maybe not the whole world, but you'd cheat for twenty kingdoms. But even then I'd still lie and say you were playing by the rules.

ALONSO

If this dream vision is typical of what this island conjures up, then I'll lose my son twice.

SEBASTIAN

A wonderful miracle!

FERDINAND

(seeing ALONSO *and kneeling)* The seas may threaten us, but they show mercy sometimes too. I cursed them for no reason.

ALONSO

Now all the blessings
Of a glad father, compass thee about.
Arise, and say how thou camest here.

MIRANDA

Oh, wonder!
How many goodly creatures are there here!
185   How beauteous mankind is! O brave new world,
That has such people in 't!

PROSPERO

'Tis new to thee.

ALONSO

(to FERDINAND*)*
What is this maid with whom thou wast at play?
Your eld'st acquaintance cannot be three hours.
Is she the goddess that hath severed us
190   And brought us thus together?

FERDINAND

Sir, she is mortal.
But by immortal providence, she's mine.
I chose her when I could not ask my father
For his advice, nor thought I had one. She
Is daughter to this famous Duke of Milan,
195   Of whom so often I have heard renown
But never saw before, of whom I have
Received a second life. And second father
This lady makes him to me.

ALONSO

I am hers.
But oh, how oddly will it sound that I
200   Must ask my child forgiveness!

PROSPERO

There, sir, stop.
Let us not burden our remembrances with
A heaviness that's gone.

ALONSO

> Receive all the blessings of a happy father. Get up and tell me how you came here.

MIRANDA

> How amazing! How many wonderful creatures there are here! Mankind is so beautiful! Oh, what a wonderful new world, that has such people in it!

PROSPERO

> It's new to you.

ALONSO

> *(to FERDINAND)* Who is this girl you were playing chess with? You can't have known her for more than three hours. Is she the goddess that separated us and then brought us back together?

FERDINAND

> No, sir, she's human. But by the grace of God, she's mine. I chose her for my wife when I thought I had no father to ask advice of. She's the daughter of this famous Duke of Milan I heard so much about but never saw before. He's given me a second life, and marrying her makes him a second father to me.

ALONSO

> And I'm her father as well. But oh, how odd it is to have to ask for my child's forgiveness!

PROSPERO

> Stop right there, sir. Let's not get gloomy in our reminiscing, since there's no reason for sadness anymore.

GONZALO
                                        I have inly wept,
         Or should have spoke ere this. Look down, you gods,
         And on this couple drop a blessèd crown,
205   For it is you that have chalked forth the way
         Which brought us hither.

ALONSO
                                        I say amen, Gonzalo.

GONZALO
         Was Milan thrust from Milan, that his issue
         Should become kings of Naples? O, rejoice
         Beyond a common joy, and set it down
210   With gold on lasting pillars. In one voyage
         Did Claribel her husband find at Tunis;
         And Ferdinand, her brother, found a wife
         Where he himself was lost; Prospero, his dukedom
         In a poor isle; and all of us, ourselves
215   When no man was his own.

ALONSO
         (*to* FERDINAND *and* MIRANDA)   Give me your hands.
         Let grief and sorrow still embrace his heart
         That doth not wish you joy.

GONZALO
                                        Be it so. Amen.

         Enter ARIEL, *with the* MASTER *and* BOATSWAIN *amazedly*
         following

         Oh, look, sir, look, sir! Here is more of us.
         I prophesied if a gallows were on land,
220   This fellow could not drown.
         (*to* BOATSWAIN)   Now, blasphemy,
         That swear'st grace o'erboard, not an oath on shore?
         Hast thou no mouth by land? What is the news?

GONZALO

I've been crying to myself just now, or I would've said the same thing. Dear gods, bless this couple, since you're the ones who have shown us the path that led us here.

ALONSO

Amen to that, Gonzalo.

GONZALO

Was the Duke of Milan kicked out of Milan so his children could become kings of Naples? Oh, this is cause for an extraordinary joy that should be engraved in gold on pillars to last forever. On one and the same trip Claribel found a husband in Tunis, and Ferdinand, her brother, found a wife where he was shipwrecked; Prospero found his dukedom on a poor island; and all of us found ourselves when we lost control of ourselves.

ALONSO

(to FERDINAND *and* MIRANDA*)* Give me your hands. May anyone who doesn't wish you joy feel grief and sorrow.

GONZALO

So be it. Amen.

ARIEL *enters with the* MASTER *and* BOATSWAIN *following in amazement.*

Oh, look, sir, look, sir! More of us are here. I remember I predicted that this guy could never drown, as long as there are gallows around on the land. *(to* BOATSWAIN*)* Hey, you curser, who defiled our ship with your foul language, don't you have any gutter talk for us on shore? What's going on?

BOATSWAIN
>   The best news is that we have safely found
>   Our king and company. The next, our ship—
> 225   Which, but three glasses since, we gave out split—
>   Is tight and yare and bravely rigged as when
>   We first put out to sea.

ARIEL
>   *(aside to* **PROSPERO***)*   Sir, all this service
>   Have I done since I went.

PROSPERO
>   *(aside to* **ARIEL***)*   My tricksy spirit!

ALONSO
>   These are not natural events. They strengthen
> 230   From strange to stranger.—
>   *(to* **BOATSWAIN***)*   Say, how came you hither?

BOATSWAIN
>   If I did think, sir, I were well awake,
>   I'd strive to tell you. We were dead of sleep
>   And—how, we know not—all clapped under hatches,
>   Where but even now with strange and several noises
> 235   Of roaring, shrieking, howling, jingling chains,
>   And more diversity of sounds, all horrible,
>   We were awaked, straightway at liberty,
>   Where we, in all her trim, freshly beheld
>   Our royal, good, and gallant ship, our Master
> 240   Capering to eye her. On a trice, so please you,
>   Even in a dream were we divided from them
>   And were brought moping hither.

ARIEL
>   *(aside to* **PROSPERO***)*   Was 't well done?

PROSPERO
>   *(aside to* **ARIEL***)* Bravely, my diligence. Thou shalt be free.

BOATSWAIN

> The best news of all is that we've located our king and
> our men. The next bit of good news is that our ship—
> which we gave up for ruined only three hours ago—is
> as well-outfitted and seaworthy as it was when we first
> set sail.

ARIEL

> *(speaking so that only* PROSPERO *can hear)* Sir, I've
> done all this work for you since I left you last.

PROSPERO

> *(speaking so that only* ARIEL *can hear)* My clever spirit!

ALONSO

> These are unnatural events. They get stranger all the
> time.—*(to* BOATSWAIN*)* Tell me, how did you get here?

BOATSWAIN

> If I were sure I was wide awake, I'd try to tell you. We
> were fast asleep and somehow—we don't know
> how—we were stowed below deck, where we heard
> lots of roaring, shrieking, howling, and jingling
> chains. The sounds were so horrible that we woke up
> liberated, and saw our wonderful ship safe and sound.
> The master was dancing with joy to see it. In an
> instant we were separated from them, as if in a dream,
> and brought here in a daze.

ARIEL

> *(speaking so that only* PROSPERO *can hear)* Did I do it
> right?

PROSPERO

> *(speaking so that only* ARIEL *can hear)* You did it per-
> fectly, my little worker. You'll get your freedom.

ALONSO
     This is as strange a maze as e'er men trod,
245   And there is in this business more than nature
     Was ever conduct of. Some oracle
     Must rectify our knowledge.

PROSPERO
                               Sir, my liege,
     Do not infest your mind with beating on
     The strangeness of this business. At picked leisure
250   Which shall be shortly, single I'll resolve you—
     Which to you shall seem probable—of every
     These happened accidents. Till when, be cheerful
     And think of each thing well.
     (aside to ARIEL*)*   Come hither, spirit.
     Set Caliban and his companions free.
255   Untie the spell.

                                       Exit ARIEL

     How fares my gracious sir?
     There are yet missing of your company
     Some few odd lads that you remember not.

     Enter ARIEL, *driving in* CALIBAN, STEPHANO, *and* TRINCULO
     in their stolen apparel

STEPHANO
     Every man shift for all the rest and let no man take care for
     himself, for all is but fortune. Coraggio, bully-monster,
260   *coraggio!*

TRINCULO
     If these be true spies which I wear in my head, here's a
     goodly sight.

CALIBAN
     O Setebos, these be brave spirits indeed!
     How fine my master is! I am afraid
265   He will chastise me.

ALONSO

This is a stranger business than men have ever set foot in before, and it's not natural either. We need some oracle to tell us what's going on.

PROSPERO

Sir, my king, don't waste your time mulling over how strange this business is. When the time is right, and it'll be soon, I promise I alone will explain everything that's happened. Until then, be cheerful and keep an open mind. *(speaking so that only* ARIEL *can hear)* Come here, spirit; set Caliban and his fellow slaves free. Break the spell that enslaves them to me.

ARIEL *exits.*

How is my lord? There are a few men still missing from the ship, a few odd guys you've forgotten about.

ARIEL *enters, driving in* CALIBAN, STEPHANO, *and* TRIN-CULO *in their stolen clothes.*

STEPHANO

Look out for the other guy, and don't put yourself first, since everything happens randomly. Courage! Courage, you fine old monster.

TRINCULO

If I can believe my eyes, this is a fine sight to see.

CALIBAN

Oh Setebos, these are handsome spirits! How wonderful my master is! I'm afraid he'll punish me.

SEBASTIAN

Ha, ha!
What things are these, my lord Antonio?
Will money buy 'em?

ANTONIO

Very like. One of them
Is a plain fish, and no doubt marketable.

PROSPERO

Mark but the badges of these men, my lords,

270   Then say if they be true.
(indicates CALIBAN*)*   This misshapen knave,
His mother was a witch, and one so strong
That could control the moon, make flows and ebbs,
And deal in her command without her power.
These three have robbed me, and this demi-devil—

275   For he's a bastard one—had plotted with them
To take my life. Two of these fellows you
Must know and own. This thing of darkness I
Acknowledge mine.

CALIBAN

I shall be pinched to death.

ALONSO

280   Is not this Stephano, my drunken butler?

SEBASTIAN

He is drunk now. Where had he wine?

ALONSO

And Trinculo is reeling ripe. Where should they
Find this grand liquor that hath gilded 'em?—
How camest thou in this pickle?

TRINCULO

285   I have been in such a pickle since I saw you last that, I fear
me, will never out of my bones. I shall not fear flyblowing.

SEBASTIAN

Why, how now, Stephano?

SEBASTIAN

Ha, ha! What are these things we're looking at, my lord Antonio? Can you buy them with money?

ANTONIO

Definitely. The one that looks like a fish is very marketable.

PROSPERO

Take a look at their servants' name tags, my lords, then tell me what they are. *(he points at* CALIBAN*)* This misshapen monster, his mother was a witch so powerful she could control the moon and the tides. These three have robbed me, and this bastard half-devil plotted with them to kill me. Two of these men you must recognize and claim as your own. This evil monster I acknowledge is mine.

CALIBAN

He'll kill me with tortures.

ALONSO

Isn't this Stephano, my drunken butler?

SEBASTIAN

He's definitely drunk now. Where did he get wine?

ALONSO

And Trinculo's drunk. Where did they find the liquor to get drunk on?—*(to* TRINCULO*)* How did you get this way?

TRINCULO

I've been so wasted since I saw you last that I'm worried I'll never be sober again. But at least I won't rot, being so full of alcohol.

SEBASTIAN

How are you doing, Stephano?

STEPHANO
> O, touch me not. I am not Stephano, but a cramp.

PROSPERO
> You'd be king o' th' isle, sirrah?

STEPHANO
290 > I should have been a sore one then.

ALONSO
> *(indicating* CALIBAN*)*
> This is a strange thing as e'er I looked on.

PROSPERO
> He is as disproportioned in his manners
> As in his shape.—*(to* CALIBAN*)* Go, sirrah, to my cell.
> Take with you your companions. As you look
295 > To have my pardon, trim it handsomely.

CALIBAN
> Ay, that I will. And I'll be wise hereafter
> And seek for grace. What a thrice-double ass
> Was I, to take this drunkard for a god
> And worship this dull fool!

PROSPERO
>   Go to, away.

ALONSO
> *(to* STEPHANO *and* TRINCULO*)*
300 > Hence, and bestow your luggage where you found it.

SEBASTIAN
> Or stole it, rather.

> *Exeunt* CALIBAN, STEPHANO, *and* TRINCULO

PROSPERO
> Sir, I invite your highness and your train
> To my poor cell, where you shall take your rest
> For this one night, which—part of it—I'll waste
305 > With such discourse as, I not doubt, shall make it
> Go quick away: the story of my life

STEPHANO

Oh, don't touch me. I'm not Stephano, I'm a walking cramp.

PROSPERO

You wanted to be king of the island, sir?

STEPHANO

I would've been a sore king then.

ALONSO

(pointing at CALIBAN*)* This is the strangest thing I ever saw in my life.

PROSPERO

He's as ugly in his manners as he is in appearance.—*(to* CALIBAN*)* Go, sir, to my room, and take your companions with you. If you want me to forgive you, make it neat and tidy.

CALIBAN

I will indeed. And after this I'll be good and hope you forgive me. What an idiot I was to think this drunkard was a god and to worship such a stupid fool!

PROSPERO

Go away, now.

ALONSO

(to STEPHANO *and* TRINCULO*)* Go, and put your garbage back where you found it.

SEBASTIAN

Or stole it, rather.

CALIBAN, STEPHANO, *and* TRINCULO *exit.*

PROSPERO

Sir, I invite your highness and your entourage to my little room, where you can sleep tonight. But for this evening—part of it, at least—I'll tell you tales to make the time pass quickly. I'll narrate the story of my life, and give you all the details of what happened to me

And the particular accidents gone by
Since I came to this isle. And in the morn
I'll bring you to your ship and so to Naples,
310 Where I have hope to see the nuptial
Of these our dear-belovèd solemnized,
And thence retire me to my Milan, where
Every third thought shall be my grave.

ALONSO

I long
To hear the story of your life, which must
315 Take the ear strangely.

PROSPERO

I'll deliver all,
And promise you calm seas, auspicious gales,
And sail so expeditious that shall catch
Your royal fleet far off.—*(aside to* ARIEL*)* My Ariel, chick,
That is thy charge. Then to the elements
320 Be free, and fare thou well!—Please you, draw near.

Exeunt omnes

since I first came to this island. And in the morning I'll take you to your ship and we'll sail to Naples, where I hope to see this loving couple married. After that I'll retire to Milan, where I'll contemplate my death, which is soon to come.

ALONSO

I'm dying to hear your life story, which must be a strange tale.

PROSPERO

I'll tell you everything, and I promise to give you calm seas and favorable winds for your trip. You'll sail so fast that you'll catch up with the royal navy.—*(speaking so that only* ARIEL *can hear)* My Ariel, baby, that job's for you. After that you'll be free as the air. Farewell!—Please, all the rest of you, come closer.

They all exit.

to self

EPILOGUE

Spoken by PROSPERO

PROSPERO
Now my charms are all o'erthrown,
And what strength I have's mine own,
Which is most faint. Now, 'tis true,
I must be here confined by you,
5   Or sent to Naples. Let me not,
Since I have my dukedom got
And pardoned the deceiver, dwell
In this bare island by your spell,
But release me from my bands
10   With the help of your good hands.
Gentle breath of yours my sails
Must fill, or else my project fails,
Which was to please. Now I want
Spirits to enforce, art to enchant,
15   And my ending is despair,
Unless I be relieved by prayer,
Which pierces so that it assaults
Mercy itself and frees all faults.
As you from crimes would pardoned be,
20   Let your indulgence set me free.

Exit

EPILOGUE

PROSPERO
Now my spells are all broken,
And the only power I have is my own,
Which is very weak. Now you all
Have got the power to keep me prisoner here,
Or send me off to Naples. Please don't
Keep me here on this desert island
With your magic spells. Release me
So I can return to my dukedom
With your help. The gentle wind
You blow with your applause
Will fill my ship's sails. Without applause,
My plan to please you has failed.
Now I have no spirits to enslave,
No magic to cast spells,
And I'll end up in despair
Unless I'm relieved by prayer,
Which wins over God himself
And absolves all sins.
Just as you'd like to have your sins forgiven,
Indulge me, forgive me, and set me free.

He exits.

SP★RKNOTES LITERATURE GUIDES

Notes

Notes

Notes

Notes

Notes

Notes

Notes